MEDITERRANEAN BOSS, CONVENIENT MISTRESS
KATHRYN ROSS

~ HIRED: FOR THE BOSS'S PLEASURE ~

HARLEQUIN®

TORONTO • NEW YORK • LONDON
AMSTERDAM • PARIS • SYDNEY • HAMBURG
STOCKHOLM • ATHENS • TOKYO • MILAN • MADRID
PRAGUE • WARSAW • BUDAPEST • AUCKLAND

Recycling programs for this product may not exist in your area.

ISBN-13: 978-0-373-52708-3
ISBN-10:   0-373-52708-X

MEDITERRANEAN BOSS, CONVENIENT MISTRESS

First North American Publication 2009.

www.eHarlequin.com

Printed in U.S.A.

"I think talk of work can wait until later..."

He brushed a finger across the smoothness of her lips. "Whereas this...can't."

His hands gently cupped her face as his head lowered toward hers. The touch of his lips against hers and the way he held her as he kissed her felt incredibly sensual and possessive. It was no gentle kiss either; it was powerfully masterful, very dominant. Charlie's senses swam with desire, and before she could think better of it, she was kissing him back with a hungry response. She was aware that his fingers moved to lace through her hair, controlling her as he thoroughly explored the sweetness of her mouth.

Charlie's emotions were all over the place as he pulled away. A part of her wanted to go back into his arms, wanted him to continue kissing her. The other part was mortified by how easily she had just capitulated to his caress, by how wantonly she had returned his kisses. *He was her boss, for heaven's sake! This could only lead to disaster.*

KATHRYN ROSS was born in Zambia, where her parents happened to live at that time. Educated in Ireland and England, she now lives in a village near Blackpool, Lancashire. Kathryn is a professional beauty therapist, but writing is her first love. As a child she wrote adventure stories, and at thirteen she was editor of her school magazine. Happily, ten writing years later, *Designed with Love* was accepted by Harlequin®. A romantic Sagittarian, she loves traveling to exotic locations.

MEDITERRANEAN BOSS, CONVENIENT MISTRESS

CHAPTER ONE

CHARLIE opened her eyes and memories from the night before flashed through her mind with agonising clarity. The date had been a complete disaster.

She hadn't really minded the fact that the man she'd met had turned out to be five feet two instead of six feet two, as he had described himself on his profile, or even the fact that he had been nearer to fifty than thirty…she wasn't ageist and she didn't think that looks were the most important things in life. However, his grey pony-tail had been a bit of a turn-off…as had the fact that they had absolutely nothing in common except that they were both divorced.

After the first fifteen minutes the date had gone rapidly downhill. Maybe internet dating wasn't a good idea. She shouldn't have allowed her friends to talk her into it.

The alarm clock rang and she reached sleepily to switch it off. A few moments later Jack came running into the bedroom. 'Time to get up, Mummy,' he sang in his usual happy tone before bounding into the bed to give her a hug.

'Morning, darling.' She kissed the top of his dark silky hair.

'Nana let me have chocolate and watch TV with her when you went out last night.'

'Did she?' Charlie smiled. 'Nana spoils you to bits.'

If it had been a weekend they would have snuggled down

for a little while and chatted. For a four-year-old Jack was a great conversationalist….probably better than her date last night, she thought with a smile. But this was Friday and there was no time for frivolity.

'Come on, then we'd better get you ready for school.'

The cottage felt cold, Charlie thought, and she put her hand on the radiator as they padded through to the bathroom. The central heating hadn't come on, which meant there was very little hot water.

Once she had dressed Jack she went to investigate the problem, but she couldn't fix it, so it was a job for the plumber again. She dreaded to think how much the repairs were going to cost.

After that there was just time for her to tie her long blonde hair back from her face, grab a piece of toast and flick through the morning post. Bills, bills and more bills…pretty much the norm. The terraced cottage was small but it cost a fortune to maintain.

At the moment Charlie was a PA and worked as a temp for an agency owned by her friend Karen. Her current position working for a doctor of psychology, who was also a best-selling author, was her most profitable assignment to date. But she still found it hard to balance her finances. The truth was that running a house and being a single mum wasn't easy and at the end of the month there wasn't a lot left over for luxuries…let alone boiler repairs!

But she would manage, she told herself firmly as they left the house. She always did.

It was a misty September morning and her old car coughed and spluttered before flaring into life. Then Jack pushed a CD into the player and they sang along with some classic love songs all the way through the rush-hour traffic.

Twenty minutes later, with Jack safely ensconced at school, she pulled back out into the traffic. She turned the volume up and hummed along to the CD as she headed for Oxford and her heart lifted. OK, so her date last night had been dreadful and there had been nothing but bills in the post, but she had the best son in the world and at the moment she was working for a very dishy boss. Just thinking about Marco Delmari gave her a little flip of anticipation.

When she had first started working for him she had instantly been attracted to his sizzling good looks. Then reluctantly her common sense had taken over and told her not to even think about it, because the job was too good to put at risk, and besides, she had priorities, she had Jack. Anyway, she realised she wasn't his type. Marco preferred stick-thin, model-perfect and incredibly glamorous women. She on the other hand was none of those things and, although she had nice hair and skin and large green eyes, unfortunately she had to wear spectacles most of the time at the office; otherwise she couldn't read the computer screen.

So not even by the flicker of an eyelash had she let him guess she thought he was gorgeous. Instead she had made herself indispensable and politely businesslike, with the result that he sang her praises, and told her how pleased he was that she had streamlined his office system and his diary. And in the last few months they had relaxed around each other and formed a repartee that was very enjoyable.

She glanced at the clock on the dashboard. Marco had to go into London to give a radio interview this morning and she wasn't sure if she'd see him before he left the office.

She took a few shortcuts down narrow, leafy lanes and arrived outside her boss's Georgian red-brick house on the outskirts of Oxford ten minutes early. His car was still parked in the courtyard and she felt a flash of exhilaration as she grabbed her briefcase and hurried up the steps to open his front door.

Her footsteps sank into the thick Persian carpets as she

hurried across the wide hallway. The house was a designer's dream, decorated in restful shades of butter-gold and cream, and furnished with stylish antiques to exactly fit the period property. But today there was no time to admire her surroundings and she went straight up the stairs to the office.

'Morning, Marco,' she said breezily as she stepped through the door and tossed her bag down on her desk. 'Beautiful day, isn't it?'

He was standing with his back towards her, looking out of the window.

'Yes, beautiful.' He turned and looked over at her, and as usual she felt a *frisson* of awareness as she met his intensely sexy dark eyes.

OK, she was relaxed around him, but not enough to stop noticing how wildly attractive he was. Marco was Italian with broodingly intense looks. His thick dark hair just brushed the collar of his blue shirt and his face was autocratically strong and handsome. The first time she had seen him was on TV and she remembered being totally taken aback by his appearance. She hadn't expected a doctor of psychology to look like him. For a start he was too young. She had pictured someone older, someone staid. The reality was a man of thirty-seven, tall, dark and powerfully built, wearing chinos and an open-necked shirt. In all honesty he had the kind of looks that a movie star would die for. Not that Marco seemed concerned about his appearance.

As soon as Charlie had started to work for him she realised that the only thing that really mattered to Marco was his work.

He had girlfriends, of course…all extremely beautiful and all crazy about him. In the short time she had worked for him she had watched them come and go, had observed how oblivious he was to their adoring looks. He really didn't have a clue how many hearts he had broken with his casual, laid-back indifference.

Marco smiled at her and a shiver of pleasure ran up her spine.
'So how was your date last night?'

His sudden question caught her off guard. She'd forgotten
she'd told him about her date. He'd casually asked about her
plans last night as she put her coat on to leave… He'd only been
making polite conversation and she could have said what she
usually said—'Nothing much'—or she could have invented
some parent meeting at Jack's school, but oh, no, she had opened
her mouth and before she knew it the truth had popped out.

'It was OK,' she answered airily now, but couldn't quite
meet his eye. She hated lying but the truth was far too embarrassing. 'Shouldn't you be getting ready to leave for the radio
station?' Swiftly she changed the subject and glanced at her
watch. Marco was due to give an interview at the BBC to
promote his new book, an analytical study into why love
shouldn't be the number-one reason for a partnership. 'If you
don't set off soon you'll be late—the traffic going into London
will be horrendous. It's Friday morning, remember.'

'Yes, I do realise that, Charlie. I'm waiting for Sarah; she
wants to accompany me in and go over a few of the questions
she thought they might ask.'

'Oh, I see.' Charlie switched on her computer. Sarah Heart
was Marco's agent and publicist, an extremely pushy woman
with an excess of confidence. Charlie found her grating. But
she was good at her job and that was all that counted, she
supposed.

'I don't know where she's got to but if she isn't here within
the next five minutes I'll have to leave without her,' Marco
muttered. He turned his back towards her again and looked out
of the window, down towards the courtyard.

'Do you want me to phone her on her mobile?'

'I've already tried that. I just got her messaging service.'

'She's probably stuck in traffic somewhere.'

'Probably.'

Charlie wondered if it was her imagination or if Marco really was unusually edgy this morning. Maybe he was just concerned about being late for this interview, although he certainly wouldn't be worried about it. Marco was very good at dealing with the media; he was always laid-back and extremely amusing and entertaining.

In fact he was much in demand on radio and TV these days and was fast becoming quite a celebrity. Academically he was brilliant and his books were always well-received, but Charlie suspected that his heightened profile and recent success was more to do with the fact that he was so captivating he even made the subject of psychology seem sexy.

There was a moment's silence as Charlie sat down at her desk and took her reading glasses out of her handbag.

'So Mr "*Dreamboat*" lived up to expectations, then?' Marco asked suddenly.

The question seemed outrageously personal and out of place in the scholarly surroundings of the book-lined office, a place where emotions were only ever discussed in the most analytical and diagnostic of terms.

'Well…' Charlie could feel her skin heating up with embarrassment as he turned and looked at her again. If it had been a mistake telling Marco about her date it had been an even bigger one telling him she'd met the man on the internet. As soon as the words were out she had imagined a hint of derision in his eyes that had made her go on to tell him that internet dating was very 'in', everyone was doing it, and the man she'd arranged to meet seemed very nice…in fact, more than nice— a bit of a dreamboat actually.

She should never have said that, she thought now with annoyance. She felt really foolish.

'Well?' Marco prompted her.

'He was OK…'

'That's good.' He inclined his head. 'I was a bit concerned.'

'You were?' She looked over at him in surprise.

'Yes. Meeting up with a total stranger can be risky.'

'I suppose so.' She was filled with a warm feeling inside. It was a long time since anyone had shown concern about her welfare. 'But I was careful; we met in a crowded restaurant and I didn't give him any of my personal details.'

'Well, I'm glad it worked out for you.'

'Actually it was a bit of a disaster,' she admitted a little awkwardly. 'We had nothing in common.'

'Oh!' Marco looked at her with a raised eyebrow. 'Not a recipe for a second date, then?'

Charlie shook her head. 'It was a struggle getting through one date, never mind two. I couldn't wait to say goodbye to him outside the restaurant.'

Marco looked amused now. 'You didn't give him much of a chance, did you?'

'I didn't need to give him any longer,' Charlie said briskly.

'I suppose not, and it's better to find out you are not compatible sooner rather than later.'

She nodded. 'Trouble was, I knew we weren't compatible within the first fifteen minutes.'

'No, you knew that the chemistry wasn't instantly there,' he corrected her. 'That's something entirely different.'

'Not to me it's not! I know your professional views on this, Marco, and I agree with them to a certain extent. Maybe love can grow if you work at a relationship, but the chemistry has to be there to start with.'

'The chemistry can be a double-edged sword,' Marco said carefully. 'Sometimes it gets in the way of the truth; blinds you to the fact that you are not at all compatible.'

'It still needs to be there to begin with.'

'Not necessarily.'

'Of course it does…I mean, you just know when you meet someone if it's going to be right…don't you?'

Marco smiled. He had a nice smile, she thought; it seemed to warm his eyes to dark golden honey. 'No. You know that you'd enjoy going to bed with them,' he said softly. 'That is an entirely different thing.'

Charlie wondered how they had got on to that subject, and suddenly felt uncomfortably hot. She always tried to keep conversations with Marco inside a safety zone, friendly but businesslike and never too personal.

'But you are right,' he continued smoothly. 'Desire can be a very important part of a relationship. It's central to a good rapport to enjoy each other in bed.'

Charlie could feel herself getting even hotter on the inside now. Marco's Italian accent had a sexy depth to it that was mesmerising, as was the way he was looking at her with those molten dark eyes. Without warning she found herself wondering what it would be like to go to bed with *him*. The question was shocking and yet at the same time wildly exciting. He would probably make a fantastic lover.

'But there is no such thing as love at first sight, if that is what you are driving at,' Marco concluded laconically.

The words drew her back to reality from the strange feelings that had taken hold of her. 'Actually, I think there is,' Charlie said staunchly. 'My parents fell in love at first sight and they were married for thirty-three years.'

Marco shook his head. 'That was lust at first sight.' He noted the look of horror in her eyes and laughed. 'Sorry to disappoint you, Charlie, but your parents would have had to get practical and work at their marriage to make it last thirty-three years.'

'It was still love at first sight,' Charlie maintained stubbornly.

Marco shook his head. 'I take it you are a bit of a romantic.'

'No!' She didn't know why she hotly denied the charge, because she *was* a hopeless romantic. Maybe it had something to do with the sudden derisive tone of his voice.

Marco watched the colour deepen in her creamy skin, saw the way her green eyes sparkled with annoyance, and smiled. 'I think you are,' he said softly. 'In fact, I think that maybe deep down you would like to find the kind of relationship that your parents enjoyed…complete with love at first sight.'

'You mean I'm looking for something you say doesn't exist,' Charlie muttered angrily. 'Any minute now you are going to ask me to lie down on your couch. I don't need to be psychoanalysed, thank you, Marco. I had a disastrous date last night but it hasn't left me scarred. I am quite well-adjusted, thank you.'

Marco laughed.

For some reason that irritated her even further.

Marco watched as she brushed a self-conscious hand over the smoothness of her hair and noticed how she swiftly changed the subject. 'You're going to be late for your interview,' she said crossly.

He smiled to himself. Charlie intrigued him and had done so since the first moment she had walked into his office. There was something about the way she carried herself with a cool dignity that was quite beguiling. Never once during the months she had worked for him had he known her to completely lower the barriers that surrounded her. However, as the weeks had gone by an easy compatibility had sprung up between them and her wary reserve had fallen a little. He noticed in particular that when he asked about her son she came alive with a warmth that was completely captivating.

On the other hand she certainly wasn't at ease talking about her date last night…watching her blush was a whole new revelation, as was the vulnerable glint in her green eyes when he had accused her of being a bit of a romantic. She had thought he'd just wanted to psychoanalyse her, but he didn't need to get her on the couch to know that some man had hurt her badly…

probably her ex-husband. But that wasn't any of his business and he certainly didn't want to pry into her personal life.

One of the things he liked about Charlie was the fact that she was so self-contained. Her practical attitude in the office was a real bonus. It suited him to have someone calm and reliable around, someone who didn't get emotional. His last PA had been a nightmare. She'd been through a series of relationship break-ups, and when he'd offered a word of sympathy she had developed a weird kind of fixation on him that had made work impossible. After that experience he had decided to hire a temp for a while. Charlie was a real blessing. She was always on an even keel, steady and dependable. Charlie never came into the office hung-over or late after a wild night on the tiles. In fact—bizarrely, considering the fact Charlie was in her late twenties and an attractive woman—she didn't appear to have a love life. Maybe he had even started to take that fact for granted… Why else had he been so taken aback when she'd told him about her date last night?

She stood up now to go and get a file from one of the cabinets and he found his eyes following her. He'd probably just been concerned about her. Sometimes, despite her self-possessed manner, he sensed an underlying vulnerability about her….something he was sure she took great trouble to hide.

Yes, that was it…he'd just been concerned for her safety last night. His attention was distracted as she reached up to a high shelf to get a new folder. For a moment he was treated to a clear view of her shapely body. As his eyes drifted down over her curves he wondered, not for the first time, why she always wore clothes that hid her physique so completely. She had a nice hourglass figure which was very desirable, but you could hardly see it in the shapeless black business suit.

Annoyed with himself, he looked away and glanced at his watch. He had more important things to think about. 'Looks like Sarah isn't going to make it. I'll have to leave without her.'

'When she arrives, shall I tell her to follow you to the studio?' Charlie asked as she sat back down at her computer.

Marco watched as she put her spectacles on and concentrated on the screen as if she had dismissed him entirely from her mind.

'No.' Marco shook his head. 'Because you'll have to come with me instead.'

She looked up at him in surprise. 'But I've got research notes to catalogue—'

'You'll have to leave them until later,' Marco said firmly. 'Come on, be quick. I need you to drive because I have notes to read. And, bearing in mind the lateness of the hour…you might have to drop me at the door and park the car for me.'

Charlie took off her spectacles and with reluctance found herself switching off her computer. Then, snatching up her bag, she followed him down the stairs. It was strange but since that conversation about her love life she felt a bit on edge around him somehow. It was as if the professional barriers that she had managed to keep in place around him had suddenly been shifted to one side.

CHAPTER TWO

CHARLIE had to practically run to keep up with Marco as they crossed the courtyard at the side of his house. She scrabbled in her bag for her keys as she stopped next to her car.

'What are you doing?'

She looked up and saw Marco was standing next to his own car.

'You said you wanted me to drive.'

'I do. But I meant in my car.'

Charlie looked over at the brand-new gleaming red sports car and quickly decided she definitely didn't want to drive such perfection through the traffic! 'Do you mind if we take mine?'

Marco glanced sceptically at her old car. 'Do you think it will get us there?'

'Well, it gets me to work every morning!' she said indignantly.

'Fine.' He shrugged and moved towards her vehicle.

Marco was so tall that his legs were crushed up against the dashboard when he got in. He released the seat and moved it backwards as she turned the key in the ignition. As usual the car didn't want to start immediately.

'It's OK—it always does this,' she reassured him hurriedly in case he started to get out.

The engine flared into life at the next turn of the key and at the same time music filled the car and Marco was treated to a rendition of *Love and Marriage* as crooned by Frank Sinatra.

Hurriedly Charlie rushed to switch it off and in her haste turned the volume up. 'Sorry!' she shouted over the sentimental words about how love and marriage went so well together and then switched the CD off. But the music kept on and it was a moment before she realised that it was the radio that was playing.

'That was Frank Sinatra's opinion of love and marriage,' The DJ said cheerfully, 'but in a short time we will be talking to the eminent Dr Marco Delmari about his new book and why he thinks putting love at the top of your list when you get married could spell disaster.'

'Sorry, I thought it was my CD that was playing,' Charlie said uncomfortably as she turned the volume down. Out of the corner of her eye she saw that Marco had found the cover for the CD of love songs and was reading through the track list.

'And you tried to tell me you weren't a romantic.' He looked over at her with wry humour.

'I've also got classical music in the glove compartment and a selection of rock albums.'

Marco smiled. 'Interesting. I wouldn't have had you down as a rock chick. Do you have the leathers and the bike too?'

'But of course,' she lied with a bat of her dark lashes. 'I didn't realise you were analysing me.'

'Of course I am.' He laughed. 'It's what I do.' He slanted her a teasing look. 'And by the way, there is nothing wrong with being a bit of a romantic,' he added softly.

'That's not what it says in your book.'

'No, what I said in my book was that people get carried away by the idea of romance. That they imagine themselves in love too easily, when in fact they are just in lust, which is absolutely fine for a short-term affair, but for a longer-term commitment you need more stability. '

'"Love should not be the only reason for marriage."' Charlie quoted one of the lines from his book.

'Ah… So you have read it, then.'

'Of course I've read it.' She looked over and found that he was still watching her with a light of amusement in his dark eyes. 'I bought a copy before I started to work for you.'

'As a precursor to internet dating?'

'No, as research towards working for you…and actually, just for the record, last night was my first sojourn into the world of internet dating.'

'Will you continue with it?'

'If you'd asked me that question when I got home last night I'd probably have said no….but…' she paused for thought '…I suppose a date like last night's can happen even when you meet someone under more conventional circumstances.'

'So you'll go out again on another date?'

Charlie shrugged. 'Maybe…'

'But not with Mr *Dreamboat*?'

'Definitely not.' She smiled at him.

Marco reached across and turned the radio off. 'So how does this internet dating service work? Do you get to see photos of the people you can date?'

'Yes, not that it helps much. My dates's photo must have been at least ten years out of date.' She glanced over at him teasingly. 'Why? Are you thinking of trying it yourself?'

'Not this week,' he said sardonically and instantly she wished she hadn't made the joke. Of course, Marco wouldn't need to look on the internet for a date—unless he was running an experiment for one of his books! But for Charlie, who didn't go out to socialise a lot—partly because she had to arrange baby-sitters, and partly because she didn't really like the nightclub or smoky-bars scene—it was a practical solution. 'It's just a bit of fun,' she said with a shrug. But her tone was defensive now.

'Is it?'

'Yes, of course.'

'So you aren't looking for a serious relationship?'

The gently asked question seemed to echo inside her in a very strange way. She had to admit that recently she had been feeling lonely and when she looked around the world suddenly seemed made up of couples. She missed the intimacy of a relationship…not just the sex but the tenderness and warmth and the feeling that someone was there for her.

Not that her ex-husband had ever really been there for her. They had only been married for twelve months when she had fallen pregnant and, although Greg initially seemed to be pleased, she had soon discovered this wasn't the case.

At the time they had been living in an apartment and had decided to look around and buy a house…something, as Greg put it, more 'child-friendly'. They had found what they were looking for pretty quickly, the ideal property; a beautiful old cottage out in the countryside.

Charlie had been ecstatic, full of dreams and plans for the future. But although their offer was accepted she had never got her dream cottage. As soon as their apartment was sold Greg had left her, taking half the money from the sale with him.

The shock had been immense. She had loved Greg and believed that he loved her, and she had never suspected for one moment that he wanted out of the marriage. Left alone and pregnant, she'd known there was no way she could afford to buy the cottage on her own, and the sale had dropped through.

So, no, she couldn't lie to herself—Greg had never been there for her…and he certainly had never bothered with Jack. That hurt more than anything.

She suddenly remembered how the other day she had seen the man next door taking his son out to play football and how for some reason it had made her eyes prickle with tears. But it had just been PMT, she told herself quickly.

She shook her negative thoughts away and answered

Marco's question. 'I don't think I want a serious relationship right now, but if someone special came along in the future that would be nice.' Charlie pulled down the visor of the car to cut the glare of sun that was so low in the sky it was shining straight into her eyes like a light of interrogation. 'Apart from anything, there are times when I think Jack needs a dad.' The words slipped out almost without her being conscious of saying them.

'Doesn't Jack see his father?'

'Not really…an occasional phone call and birthday card…' She glanced over at Marco and suddenly felt completely self-conscious when she found he was watching her with a very serious expression in his eyes. Why was she telling him this? It was none of his business! 'However, he's no great loss,' she added hastily. 'And I like my independence. I'd certainly rather be on my own than in a bad relationship.'

'Very wise,' Marco said with a nod.

'Anyway, I'm distracting you from your work,' she said briskly, trying to change the subject. 'You should be reading your notes.'

'Yes, I suppose I should.'

Silence descended between them. Charlie felt awkward now as he shuffled through papers. She wished she hadn't had that conversation. She had to work with the guy and it was always best to keep personal conversations to a minimum and maintain a cool and businesslike front. The strange thing was that recently she had been finding that more and more diffi-cult. Marco was very easy to talk to…but then he would be, she thought suddenly; he was trained to get people to open up and reveal their innermost feelings.

After a few moments she felt his eyes resting on her again. Why did she feel that he was looking at her with closer atten-tion than usual? She glanced over at him questioningly.

'Sorry, was I staring?' He shook his head. 'I just realised

that you are not wearing your spectacles. Don't you need them for driving?'

'No, it's OK.' She smiled and looked back at the road. 'I'm not going to crash the car. I'm glad to say I only need them in the office for the close paperwork and the computer.'

'You look different without them.'

'I know…they don't suit me, do they?'

'Actually—'

Charlie was glad that the ring of Marco's phone interrupted the conversation at that moment. She didn't want him to politely lie and tell her that her glasses did suit her because in retrospect it sounded as if she had been fishing for compliments, which certainly wasn't the case.

She watched out of the side of her eye as he took the phone from his inside jacket pocket and flipped it open.

'Hi, Sarah; where the heck are you?' he demanded. 'Really?' He smiled. 'No, Charlie was good enough to drive me in. We'll be about twenty minutes.' He listened for a moment to something she had to say. 'I don't think that will be a problem because I've done the research. The facts speak for themselves.' Marco's voice held a dry edge now. He was clearly irritated by something. 'We'll talk about it later…OK?' Then he hung up.

'Problems?' Charlie asked, overcome with curiosity.

'Yes, the problem is that sometimes Sarah can be very irritating,' he said tersely.

Those were Charlie's sentiments exactly, but she wondered what Sarah had said to aggravate Marco. The pair usually seemed to get on so well, sometimes almost sickeningly so. Many times Charlie had watched as Sarah fawned over him, agreeing with his every word, fluttering her eyelashes coyly and then basking in his attention. There was no doubt in Charlie's mind that the woman fancied the pants off him, and Marco had never seemed averse to the attention.

They had left the motorway now and Charlie followed the

signs for the city centre. 'You need to turn left down here,' Marco said as they approached a busy junction.

'Where is Sarah anyway?' Charlie asked as she negotiated the traffic.

'She's had a crisis on her hands. Apparently one of her celebrity clients has confronted her husband's mistress in the lingerie department of Harrods and has been arrested for making a public disturbance.'

'Really?'

Marco nodded. 'Sarah's had to rush down to the police station to get her out before the Press get wind of it.'

'Never a dull moment in her profession.'

'You can say that again. Yesterday she was trying to talk me into getting married, or at least getting into a monogamous long-term relationship.'

Charlie shot him a startled look. She was so surprised she nearly ran a red light and just put the brakes on in time.

'It's her latest business idea apparently.'

'A business idea?' Charlie was nonplussed.

'Yes. As you know, my book is due to be released in America soon and I'm going on tour to promote it. It's already getting a lot of coverage; magazines and chat shows are discussing my ideas. So it should shoot in high in the book charts.'

'That's good. But I still don't see where Sarah's idea fits in with this.'

'Sarah thinks that the fact that I am a bachelor will substantially affect sales. And that I might not make the number-one slot because of it.'

'That's ridiculous. It's a scientific book, not one written from a personal angle. It uses statistics, case studies and research projects.'

'Exactly. I said all this to Sarah last night. But she still thinks that if I were committed to someone it would give the book vital credence. We had quite a disagreement about it.'

'She's unbelievable,' Charlie muttered and at the same time she wondered if there was method in Sarah's madness. Perhaps she had herself in mind to be on the arm of her darling doctor? 'It's just absurd.'

'Well…' Marco shrugged. 'I suppose if I did get together with someone I could prove my research that love isn't the most important prerequisite for a successful relationship. However…' he grinned '…I'm not entirely sure I approve of Sarah's suggestion and I told her that.'

Charlie nodded emphatically and enjoyed picturing the dis-appointment on Sarah Heart's face as Marco disagreed with her. Sarah was undoubtedly very beautiful but she had all the warmth of the dark side of the moon. It was somehow gratify-ing to know that the woman didn't get everything she wanted.

Marco directed her down some side-streets and a few seconds later they turned through the gates into the radio station. A security guard raised the barrier and allowed them in. 'Will you park the car, Charlie?' Marco asked as he looked at his watch. 'I should go straight in.'

'Yes, of course.' She pulled to a halt by the front door. 'Do you want me to wait for you out here?'

'No, come in and get a coffee.' He reached for the handle and stepped out of the car. 'I'll tell the receptionist to expect you.'

Charlie noticed how a young woman walking towards the building gave him an admiring look. He said something to her and then held the door so that she could precede him into the building. She looked as if she was going to swoon. It was no wonder, because he really was drop-dead gorgeous, Charlie thought dreamily. Everything about him was sexy, from the way he dressed…to the way he just looked at you as if he could unlock the secrets of your soul. It was little wonder that Sarah Heart had designs on him.

Realising that she was just sitting staring after him, Charlie shook herself out of her contemplation and drove the car around the back of the building to park. Then she collected her bag and walked towards the front entrance.

As she reached the front door a taxi pulled up. The door of the vehicle opened and a pair of high black stiletto boots and long, shapely legs swung out. As Charlie's gaze moved upwards she saw a red skirt, and then as the woman uncurled herself from the car completely a long black cashmere coat swirled around her. It was Sarah Heart and as usual she looked very glamorous, her long brunette hair shimmering with cappuccino highlights in the sun, the perfect proportions of her face flawlessly made-up with a light smudging of gold frosted shadow over her dark eyes and a glossy shimmer of ruby-red on the fullness of her lips.

'Hello, Sarah.' Charlie stood and waited for her.

'Hi.' The woman gave her what could only be described as a look of dismissal before turning to pay the taxi driver. Charlie was tempted to just walk into the studio without her, but she forced herself to wait.

'Did you manage to spring your celeb client from jail?' she asked as the woman turned to walk with her into the building.

'Yes, thank you, although it is a confidential matter that I'd rather Marco hadn't mentioned to you.'

'Well, maybe you shouldn't have told him in the first place then.' Charlie couldn't resist the retort. Really, the woman could be most disagreeable.

Sarah ignored that. 'Is Marco already in the building?' she continued, unperturbed.

'Yes, he went on ahead.'

'Good…well, I suppose there is little point in you hanging around, then, not now that I'm here.'

'Marco has asked me to stay,' Charlie said firmly. She wasn't about to be dismissed in such a manner.

'I thought you might have typing to get on with,' the woman shrugged, 'or some filing perhaps.'

Charlie wondered if Sarah practised that condescending tone or if it just came naturally to her. She decided to ignore the remark and followed her towards the front desk.

Sarah nodded at the receptionist. 'I'm here with Marco Delmari,' she said in a crisply confident tone.

'And your name?' The receptionist looked down at the register in front of her.

'Sarah Heart.' Sarah drummed one well-manicured hand against the desk as she waited.

'I'm sorry, Ms Heart, but I don't appear to have your name on my list.'

'I beg your pardon?' Sarah looked as if she was about to turn an interesting shade of purple.

Before she could launch into a scathing remark Charlie leaned across her. 'Excuse me, but have you got my name on the list? It's Charlotte Hopkirk,' she said quietly.

The woman ran her eyes over the book again. 'Oh, yes, your name is here, Ms Hopkirk.'

'Good, well, this is Dr Delmari's publicist, so she should be down as well.'

'I see.' The girl smiled at Charlie. 'Then I guess it's OK for her to accompany you through. You'll find Dr Delmari in the hospitality suite next door to studio five, the door should be open.'

'Thank you.'

'What on earth are you thanking her for?' Sarah muttered as they moved away from the desk. 'She was clearly incompetent.'

'Your name wasn't down, so it was hardly her fault. Anyway no harm done; it's just a good job that I stayed with you,' Charlie couldn't resist adding.

Sarah slanted her a narrow-eyed look but said nothing.

They found Marco talking to the station manager. He smiled over at Charlie as she walked through the door. Then he turned his attention to his publicist. 'Sarah, this is a surprise! There was no need for you to rush down here.'

'I wanted to, Marco. I'm so sorry I was held up,' she said smoothly. Charlie noticed how her voice had softened now that she was talking to Marco. Then she flashed a winning smile at the station manager. 'Sarah Heart,' she said as she extended her hand. 'Marco's publicist.'

'Pleased to meet you, Ms Heart.'

'Call me Sarah, please,' she practically purred.

'Well, Sarah, we are just waiting for our DJ Sam Richmond to come through and have a word with Marco then we'll go through to the studio.'

'How is Sam?' Sarah gushed. 'It's a while since I saw him.'

'You're a friend?' the station manager asked.

'Oh, yes, Sam and I go way back.'

He was probably ex-husband number three, Charlie thought darkly. According to gossip Sarah had been married and divorced four times, which was no mean feat by the age of thirty-eight. Ex-husband number four had been a top TV executive and a wealthy man. It was through his contacts and money that Sarah had started her business.

The DJ came in at that moment and Sarah made a performance out of greeting him and introducing him to Marco. She probably wouldn't have bothered to include Charlie only Sam Richmond smiled at her and reached to shake her hand.

'Oh, and that's Charlie,' she tagged on, her tone less than gracious. 'She's—'

'My right-hand woman,' Marco finished the sentence smoothly.

Charlie caught Marco's eye and he smiled at her. Something about that smile made her feel warm and special. It was a delicious feeling. She almost had to shake herself to get rid of its dreamy effect.

A few moments later she was left alone in the hospitality suite as Sarah accompanied the men through to the studio. Charlie poured herself a coffee from a pot that was sitting on the sideboard and sat down in one of the comfortable armchairs to wait. She could see the others through the glass partition between her and the studio next door but she couldn't hear what they were saying, she could only hear the record that was being played on air.

She found herself watching Marco, studying him as he talked. She liked the sincerity in his eyes as he listened to people, and she noticed that when he smiled he had a dimple in his cheek. As she glanced away her eyes connected with Sarah's and she knew the other woman had caught her watching her boss. Hastily she looked away feeling guiltily uncomfortable…although for the life of her she couldn't work out why.

She had just got up to replenish her coffee when Sarah joined her. 'I'll have one of those while you're there,' she told Charlie as she sat down. 'White, no sugar.'

Charlie poured her the drink and handed it across. She noticed how Sarah didn't even bother to say thank you. She really was quite rude, Charlie thought with annoyance.

Sarah watched as she sat back down in her chair opposite. 'So…' she murmured idly as she crossed her long legs and smoothed down the silky material of her skirt, 'tell me, Charlie…how long have you been in love with Marco?'

The outrageously personal question was asked with such nonchalance that for a moment Charlie wondered if she had misheard. 'What on earth are you talking about?' She stared at the woman in astonishment.

'I think you know,' Sarah continued smoothly.

'All I know is that you are asking me an absurd question!'

'Am I?' Sarah shrugged. 'From where I'm watching it seems blindingly obvious that you have a thing for him.'

Charlie was so outraged that she could barely find her voice. 'I'm not even going to deign to answer that!' she finally muttered.

'You know you aren't his type, don't you?' Sarah smiled but

her eyes were cold. 'And I'm not just talking about the fact that Marco only seems to date women who look like super-models, I'm talking about the fact that Marco would never fall for a romantic. He's far too practical for that. So I'm afraid that unless you take those rose-coloured glasses off when you look at him…I think you have a problem.'

The sardonic tone grated on Charlie. 'I think the only problem around here is you,' she said succinctly. 'And I'll thank you to keep your weird opinions to yourself.'

Sarah just laughed.

At that moment the music stopped and the radio interview started. Charlie tried to switch off from the preposterous accusations and concentrate on the conversation in the studio but Sarah's words kept echoing around in her mind with disturbing emphasis.

How long have you been in love with Marco?

CHAPTER THREE

'ARE you OK?' Marco's quiet tone cut across the silence in the car.

'Absolutely fine.' Charlie changed gear with a grating sound that exactly mirrored the way she was feeling inside.

'You haven't spoken much since leaving the radio studio.'

Because she couldn't believe the audacity of Sarah Heart—imagine asking a question like that! If anyone was in love with Marco Delmari it was Sarah herself. The woman had been almost sycophantic towards Marco as they were leaving the station. She'd invited him over to her apartment for dinner on Sunday, ostensibly to discuss his American tour, but by the tone of her voice she'd had more in mind than business discussions…and Marco had accepted the invitation quite happily. But maybe the thing that had annoyed her most of all was the way Sarah had looked at her as Marco accepted Sarah's invitation. There had been triumph and disdain in the other woman's eyes, as if to say *you will never hook a man like Marco Delmari.*

'Well, you know me, I'm always quiet,' Charlie murmured as she realised Marco was waiting for a reply. 'The interview went well,' she said, trying to change the direction of her thoughts. She wasn't in love with Marco and it didn't matter what Sarah Heart thought.

'Yes,' Marco frowned. 'Except for the questions about my love life; I didn't think they were relevant.'

'No, they weren't, but I suppose he had to ask. People will be interested in your private life.'

'You are starting to sound like Sarah,' Marco said drily.

'Sorry!' The last thing she wanted was to sound like Sarah Heart!

'That's OK. Maybe on reflection she has a point.'

Charlie glanced over at him in horror. 'No she hasn't!'

Marco smiled. 'From an academic's point of view she hasn't. However, I'm not aiming my book solely at academics. It's for the mass market and I have to give Sarah her due, she is a good businesswoman. She knows how to work the media…knows what sells.'

Charlie wanted to correct him and tell him that Sarah Heart just had her eye on the main chance…that she fancied a sexy doctor as husband number five. But she pulled herself back. 'You're not considering her idea of entering into a relationship as…as some kind of a publicity stunt, are you?' she asked instead, her tone laced with incredulity.

'Well, I'm still not completely convinced. But I suppose having a partner around at the moment wouldn't go amiss.' He shrugged. 'But it would have to be somebody who is on a similar wavelength to me—'

'You mean someone who wouldn't get carried away by it all and imagine herself in love with you?' Charlie guessed wryly.

'No, I mean someone who believes in my ideas,' Marco corrected her pointedly. 'However, as my book tour starts in just a few weeks, I'd have to be quick to find a suitable candidate in that time.'

'Oh, I'm sure you would be able to dig up someone acceptable very quickly,' Charlie murmured. *Sarah Heart* for one, she thought sardonically.

The edge in her voice wasn't lost on Marco. 'The idea of a

relationship without love really offends your sense of romance, doesn't it?'

'No. I just have doubts that it would work out in the long term.'

'What kind of doubts?'

'Well, you know…that it would actually *last.*'

'Of course it will,' Marco said softly. 'I've backed up the hypothesis with exhaustive research studies. If two people are serious about wanting to get married…or about making a long-term commitment…and they follow the steps I've outlined in the book, then the relationship should be successful regardless of whether they are in love or not, the main proviso being both parties are willing to work at the agreement.'

'It doesn't sound very romantic. I always thought that all Italians were incredibly impulsive and passionate,' Charlie murmured thoughtfully. 'But you don't really fit the criteria… do you?'

'What makes you think that?' Marco gave her a half-smile that made her tingle with sudden awareness of him. 'Being impulsive and passionate with someone is one thing…making a lifelong commitment to them is quite another.'

'Well…yes…obviously…' Charlie was mortified now; she wished she hadn't said that. 'I was just talking about the romantic side of a partnership.'

'But that is my whole point. For a relationship to be successful you're supposed to work at that side of things as well.'

'But if you are both in love to begin with, surely romance follows naturally like night follows day.'

'Nice theory.' Marco smiled at that. 'But unfortunately not true. Very often love is just an illusory feeling…a misleading mirage…and even if it is not you can't rely totally on just that feeling to sustain a relationship over the long term. You need to look deeper than that.'

Charlie looked over at him wryly. 'Maybe you just don't believe in love.' She couldn't resist the comment.

'When making a long-term commitment I think it is an emotion that should be approached with caution.' Marco's voice was dry. 'All too often people confuse making love with being in love…two different things entirely. It's fine to have wild nights of passion and not think too deeply about things. But before you make any promises you should think with your head, not your heart.'

'Sometimes you sound more cynical than sensible.'

'I'm just a realist, Charlie.' He shrugged. 'I believe if you are looking for a successful long-term relationship it's best to be practical, not starry-eyed. And, as bizarre as it sounds, my findings are that if you can disregard love from the equation you can see a relationship more clearly. But maybe the theory wouldn't be successful for someone like you.'

'What do you mean, someone like me?' Charlie pulled the car to a halt in front of his house and turned to look at him.

'Well…' he shrugged in that particular way of his '…you're obviously an incurable romantic.'

'I wish you would stop saying that.' Charlie glared at him.

'Sorry, Ms Hopkirk.' His tone was teasing. 'But that is my considered opinion and the prognosis isn't good, I'm afraid. There's no hope for you.'

Unfortunately Charlie failed to see the humour behind his words. 'Well, that is where you are wrong…*actually.*' She emphasised the word with derision. 'I was cured from my…as you would term…*delusional* state a long time ago. I got divorced and became a single parent. That has a way of grounding the senses, believe me.'

'Hey, I was just making a light-hearted remark!' Marco held up his hands and looked at her with that glint in his eye that she was starting to recognise so well.

'No you weren't, you were being condescending. Well, yes, I do like roses, soft, honeyed words and moonlight…but I'm not so stupid that I would fall in love and get married just because they are applied to a situation. And let me tell you, I'm looking for something much more realistic next time around, believe me.'

'Are you?'

The sudden interest in his tone pulled her up and made her realise that she had just lost her temper, but why she had got so steamed up she didn't know. Maybe because she was still smarting from Sarah's earlier remarks, or maybe it was because she didn't like the idea that Marco seemed to think that she was some kind of dreamer who had completely unrealistic expectations of life and wasn't to be taken seriously. Just because she believed in true love and romance didn't mean she was bewildered. Well, perhaps this was her chance to prove—even if she did have to lie a little bit! 'Of course I want something realistic. I've made one mistake in my life by choosing the wrong partner and I don't want to make another,' she answered him hesitantly. 'Sorry to disappoint you but my days of being starry-eyed are long gone. Deep down I am also a realist.'

'So are you saying that if the terms were right you wouldn't be averse to the idea of a serious relationship based on common sense rather than love?' Marco continued wryly.

'Terms?' Charlie frowned.

'Marriage, or cohabitation, should be treated like a business partnership; you need to know exactly what you want out of it before you enter into it.' Marco noticed the high colour on her cheekbones and smiled. 'You see…you do find the idea too clinical…distasteful even. I rest my case.'

'No! If the terms were right I might consider such an idea.' She raised her head defiantly. She wasn't going to back down.

Marco gave her a sardonic smile. 'Well I don't believe you…I think your heart would be far too soft and emotional to ever be happy with that kind of an arrangement.'

'And what are you basing that opinion on?' Charlie asked dismissively. 'The fact that I listen to romantic music?'

'No…I'm basing it on what you have told me about yourself…about your parents' marriage…about your date last night.'

'You don't know anything about me.' Charlie shrugged. 'But believe what you want! Now…I think we should forget this nonsense and get back to work.' She tried to switch the subject and reached for the door handle, but Marco touched her arm, stopping her from getting out of the car.

'So what *are* you looking for in your next relationship?'

The blunt question took her completely by surprise. She looked back at him and as she met the seriousness of his dark eyes she realised that perhaps this conversation had gone a little too far. 'Well….I….hadn't really thought about it that deeply. I mean…I was only speaking hypothetically.'

He was looking at her very intently as if he could see into her very soul…see the romantic streak lurking beneath the surface. And to her dismay she felt herself blushing wildly. This wasn't fair—he had no right to ask such personal questions!

Marco laughed. 'A word of warning, Charlie; never try and play poker, you wouldn't be much good.'

It was that derisive, cynical laugh that pushed her over the edge. 'Well, OK, then, if you really want to know, next time around I'd want…companionship.' She pulled the word wildly out of mid-air.

'Companionship?' He didn't know whether to believe her or not. She could see the dark light in his eyes was tinged with just a hint of uncertainty.

'Well yes…' She held his dark gaze determinedly. 'What's the matter—isn't that practical enough for you?'

'We're not talking about me…we are talking about you and what *you* would want,' Marco corrected her softly. 'And would companionship really be enough for you?'

She wished those dark eyes of his weren't so intense…

Companionship would be good but she knew deep down it would never be enough for her. She would want a deep and passionate love…nothing less would suffice. She wished she'd never stated this lie now. Charlie glanced away from him. 'Obviously the guy would have to care deeply about Jack and be good with him.' She added the provision hastily. That at least was the truth.

'Obviously.' Marco nodded.

'As you said in your book, it's important not to allow emotions to cloud reality.' She threw the line in for good measure.

'You have been paying attention.' He smiled.

She frowned; was he being facetious? 'No, I've been through a divorce and, as I said before, it has a way of grounding the senses. Why do you think I've chosen internet dating? Let's face it; it is the ultimate practical way to meet someone. You read through a list of a person's attributes and decide from that if you have something in common. There are no hearts and flowers about choosing a partner using that method, I assure you.' She left out the fact that it had been her friend Karen who had talked her into it.

'I guess so.' Marco frowned for a moment. 'Maybe you are a little more practical than I gave you credit for.'

'A *lot* more practical,' she corrected him quickly. Even though she veered towards the romantic, that didn't mean she wasn't sensible.

Marco held up his hands. 'Obviously I was very wrong in my assessment of you.'

'Yes, you were.' She smiled, pleased with the new note of respect in his tone. And now she knew why she had felt so compelled to lie. The label of incurable romantic was not a good one to have around Marco.

His eyes swept over her thoughtfully. He'd always had Charlie down as someone who could never view a relationship in just practical terms, but now that she had convinced him otherwise perhaps she was just what he needed… 'So, now that we have established the fact that we are both on a similar wavelength…so to speak…how about shelving your internet-dating idea for a while and coming out to dinner with me?'

The question was asked so nonchalantly that for a moment Charlie wondered if she had misheard. 'I beg your pardon?'

'I was asking you out for dinner…you know, the meal that comes after lunch and before bed.'

The teasing, provocative words caused Charlie's heart to slam hard against her chest. She didn't know how to take this sudden turn of conversation at all. 'As in…a date?'

'Yes…as in a date,' Marco said softly and suddenly his tone was very serious.

As their eyes met Charlie felt a flare of pure sexual attraction so raw it took her breath away. She couldn't deny that she was wildly attracted to him. Then common sense kicked in as she reminded herself that Marco was not only her boss but also a man who only dated women who looked as if they'd come straight off a catwalk.

She tilted up her chin. 'And why would you do that?'

Marco noted the expression of surprise and consternation in her eyes.

'Why not?' he countered quietly.

'Well, for one thing, you're my boss and it's not good to mix business with pleasure.' She decided to concentrate on practicalities, with her words stiff and formal.

'I didn't realise you were so conventional.' His mouth slanted in a half-smile.

'I was being sensible.'

'Well, as you know, I'm all for being sensible.' He regarded her with a wry, teasing gleam in his eye. 'But you've intrigued me now and I want to find out more about this deeply practical side of your nature and what you are searching for in your next relationship.'

'I'm not really searching for anything!' Charlie said hurriedly.

'That's not what you just said.'

'I was just speaking hypothetically….just…you know… proving that my poker skills are better than yours.'

'But you told me that you were specifically looking for a realistic type of relationship.' Marco murmured the words silkily, knowing how she would react. 'I kind of got the impression that you might have been sussing me out…testing the water…finding out if I was up for the idea.'

'I certainly was not!' Charlie was furious. 'How could you think such a thing?'

'Very easily when you are laying out your requirements in such an open and honest way.'

'Oh, for heaven's sake…' Charlie trailed off as she suddenly noticed the glint of devilment in his dark eyes. 'Are you winding me up?' she asked suspiciously.

'Just a little…' He smiled and his eyes moved over her countenance thoughtfully.

Something about the way he was looking at her made her feel extremely self-conscious. 'Well, I think the joke has gone far enough.' She glanced away from him, feeling foolish now. 'We should get back to work—'

'Hey, not so fast.' He put a hand on her arm as she made to turn away from him again. 'You still haven't given me your answer. Will you have dinner with me?'

She turned back and regarded him with a frown. 'I told you the joke has gone far enough, Marco.'

'I wasn't joking about dinner,' he said quietly.

He watched the scepticism flicking through her eyes. 'Of course I was serious,' he added gently. 'I told you…you've intrigued me.'

She noticed how his gaze moved over her with leisurely appraisal. There was something in its warmth that touched her defences for a second. 'And why is that?' she asked huskily before she could stop herself.

'Well, for one thing, it's very rare that I meet a woman who views relationships in my level-headed terms.'

The matter-of-fact answer snapped her quickly back to reality. 'Let me guess. You want to get inside my brain to research a woman's take on practicality.' She tried to sound flippant, but deep down she was aware of an irrational curl of hurt. She knew he wasn't asking her out for her beauty, but did he have to be so blunt about it?

'I wouldn't have worded it quite like that,' he contradicted her softly. For a moment his eyes drifted down over the soft curves of her body.

In fact, whom was he kidding? he thought drily. He wouldn't put it like that at all. Perhaps the reason he had been so concerned about her internet dating last night was more complex than he'd first thought. He was a man who had a healthy sexual appetite and during the last couple of days he had been surprised to find that there was something about the way she looked at him sometimes…the way she moved…that turned him on. But, as she so rightly had pointed out a few moments ago, business and pleasure did not mix.

He had mockingly accused her of being conventional for having such sentiments, but in truth weren't they part of the reason he had felt so at ease around Charlie these last few months? After the uncomfortable atmosphere his last PA had generated it had been great to be around someone who thought like him and wanted to keep the working environment strictly complication-free. In fact he had been so at ease with Charlie that he had enjoyed trying to draw her out from behind those reserved barriers of hers, and now somehow he had managed to become interested in her sexually. Being interested in her in that way was not the prudent and practical thing to do. But…now he was starting to revise that opinion.

The clinical part of his mind had clicked on when she had talked about finding something more realistic for her next relationship. Maybe there was an opportunity for business and pleasure to mix very well indeed here… Maybe it would be OK to pursue Charlie…maybe…in practical terms she was just what he needed right now.

'Perhaps we should try each other out for size.' His eyes drifted back towards her face.

The sudden change of tack took her by surprise. There was something almost hypnotic about the smoothly sensual Italian tones. 'Now you are just being…' Charlie struggled to find the right word. She could hardly think straight when he looked at her like that '…outrageous.'

'Am I?' He smiled. 'You were talking earlier this morning about chemistry… There is more than a *frisson* of that between us…don't you think?'

'No!' She cut across him abruptly. He was moving into dangerous territory now that she didn't want to analyse.

Her eyes were drawn to his lips…they were curved in a derisive smile…but they were also sexily inviting. Was it her imagination or was he very close? She could smell the tang of his aftershave, fresh and very inviting.

She noticed that his eyes were on her lips. Unconsciously she moistened them with the tip of her tongue. A strong feeling of desire suddenly laced the air between them. It was so heavy that Charlie could feel it thundering through her, making her heart race, twisting a latent need into life with shocking force.

In that instant she wanted him to kiss her—no, more than that, she wanted him to take her into his arms and make passionate love to her…

The knowledge rang alarm bells inside her but she couldn't stem the feelings, they were flowing through her with the most amazing force. She couldn't remember the last time a man had turned her on so completely like this without even touching her!

'How about I pick you up tonight about seven?'

The smooth words were more of an order than a suggestion. He really was insufferably sure of himself, Charlie thought hazily, and really she should tell him right now that she had other plans.

But for some reason the words just wouldn't come out. She swallowed hard as he reached out a hand and touched the side of her face; although his fingers were a whisper-soft caress against her skin, she felt them with such a pleasurable, forceful intensity that involuntarily she closed her eyes.

Charlie wanted that caress to go on and on, it was as if she were falling into a very deep, spiralling trap with nowhere to go except towards the light of desire and need. She had never felt like this before, it was as if she wasn't in control of her own senses…it was scary and yet it was wonderful at the same time.

Then Marco pulled back, leaving her shaking and breathless.

'So I'll see you tonight, yes?'

His voice was so arrogantly cool and calm that it brought her back to her senses as sharply as if he had slapped her. Shocked by the intensity of her disappointment because he hadn't kissed her, she struggled to pull herself together.

'We've got to work together, Marco,' she murmured reprovingly.

'Yes.' He nodded and then grinned. 'Have I ever told you that I like that prim and proper attitude of yours? It's very refreshing.'

'It's not supposed to be refreshing, it's supposed to be sensible.'

He smiled. 'You're talking my language again.' He glanced at his watch. 'And yes, I agree there are things we need to discuss…sensibly. Unfortunately there is no time now. It will have to wait until tonight.'

She shook her head…mesmerised by his determined

attitude. 'I couldn't get someone to look after Jack tonight. It's too short notice—'

'OK, lunch tomorrow.' He cut across her nonchalantly. 'I'll pick you up at about twelve-thirty.'

'Marco…' But she didn't have time to say anything else because he had turned and opened the car door to step out into the bright afternoon sunlight.

This really was preposterous, Charlie thought as she grabbed for the door handle and stepped out after him. 'I am not going on a date with you, Marco!'

'Why not?'

Why not indeed? As Charlie looked across at his tall handsome physique she was asking herself the same question and weakness started to invade. With determination she raised her chin and forced herself to be level-headed. She couldn't go out with him because he was her boss, she reminded herself sharply. Business and pleasure didn't go together. And added to that he was only interested in her now because she had lied to him about the type of person she was. He had admitted earlier that it would help endorse his theories and his book to have a girlfriend around for a while who thought the same way he did. Well, that position definitely wouldn't suit her!

'Because…it wouldn't work out,' she told him firmly.

'I told you earlier, Charlie, in order to find out if something will be successful you have to give it a chance.' He shrugged. 'However, you can relax, there are a few work-related issues I'd like to discuss with you anyway. So tomorrow would be a good chance to do that.'

'What kind of work issues?'

'We'll discuss that tomorrow.' He glanced at his watch. 'I've got to get over to St Agnes Hospital now to deal with two referrals.'

He sounded very calm and assured and it was light-years

away from how she was feeling. She was utterly confused. Had tomorrow's lunch date just been relegated to a business meeting?

'So let me get this right; you told your boss that you weren't averse to having an intimate relationship with him based on compatibility alone and he suddenly asked you out?' Karen was sitting at the kitchen table analysing the story.

'I didn't mention the word intimate,' Charlie corrected her quickly. 'And I wasn't talking about having a relationship with *him*, I was just talking hypothetically! He took my words out of context.'

'Hmm.' Karen looked at her with a raised eyebrow.

'I was just trying to convince him that I'm not a hopeless romantic.' Charlie tried to make light of the subject.

She had phoned her friend Karen as soon as she got home from work because she had felt she needed to talk about what had happened. Karen had then come straight around to her house to go over it all again, and Charlie wished now she hadn't mentioned it; it was all too uncomfortable.

'Because Sarah Heart accused you of being in love with him?'

'Well, that was part of it, the other part was that Marco can be quite condescending when it comes to people who are…emotional rather than practical.' She put a pot of tea down on the kitchen table between them and sat down again. 'Anyway, let's just forget about it, shall we? It's all rubbish. I've no intention of going out with Marco on a date.'

'Why not?' Karen leaned back in her chair. 'Going by what I've seen of him on TV, he is quite a dish.'

'Yes, he's very good-looking.' Charlie shrugged. 'But he's my boss and…well, for a start, we think differently; he doesn't believe that love is the most important thing in a relationship and I do.'

'So you lied…so what?' Karen shrugged. 'It's a mere formality anyway.'

'Not to Marco it's not. I told you he's very serious about viewing a relationship in a purely practical way.'

'Well, if I were in your shoes I'd just continue to pretend that I was Ms Practicality. He doesn't need to know that your favourite film is *Sleepless in Seattle*…does he?'

Charlie laughed.

'And he's only your boss for another month—then your contract is finished,' Karen reminded her succinctly. She raked a hand through her short brown hair. 'You could risk a short involvement with him to see how things go.'

'And let him think that I was propositioning him when I said I'd consider a relationship based on practicalities…because that is what he thinks, you know. The guy is pretty big-headed.' Charlie shook her head. 'Anyway, I've already turned him down so it's too late for all that. If we go out tomorrow it will be to discuss work. He's quite happy with that. His interest in me is businesslike anyway. '

'You're just frightened of getting hurt again, aren't you?' Karen observed suddenly. 'You can't keep hiding yourself away like this, Charlie. You've been doing that since your divorce. You've got to get out there again.'

'I know.' Charlie reached out and poured the tea. 'But I don't think Marco is the right person for me. Now, let's change the subject. I don't want to think about him a moment longer. How are things at the agency?'

To Charlie's relief Karen let it drop. 'Actually they are a bit chaotic.'

Charlie was on the books of Karen's employment agency and knew only too well that things were manic in there. From time to time in between contracts she went in to help her friend run the place and it was an arrangement that suited them both. Karen got extra help from someone she could trust implicitly, which meant she could take some time off to be with her children, and Charlie got a job to fill some of the gaps between her temping contracts.

'It's peaks and troughs, it will calm down next week probably,' Charlie said soothingly.

'Maybe.' Karen put her cup down. 'But I'm seriously considering selling the place, Charlie. You know I told you I'd had a take-over bid from a rival agency?'

Charlie nodded. Her friend had been stressed for a while trying to balance her home life with work and had talked about selling last month, but hadn't been offered enough money.

'Well, they've upped the offer.'

'That's really good, Karen!'

'Yes, except for one thing: I think they will close my office here. They are a big company and basically they are just interested in squeezing out the competition and covering contracts with their own people.'

'I see.' Charlie felt a pang of apprehension as she realised this probably wasn't going to bode well for her future work. Then, seeing the worried expression on her friend's face, she quickly pulled herself together. 'Karen you must do what is right for you,' she said sincerely.

'I just hate the thought that this isn't going to work well for my staff,' Karen said with a shrug. 'And then there is you. You've always been so brilliant at bailing me out in the office—'

'Karen, nothing stays the same in life, and I'm probably lucky to have got away with temping for as long as I have.' Charlie smiled and topped up her tea. 'Whatever you decide, I'll be behind you,' she said firmly. 'Don't worry about me. I'm a survivor.'

CHAPTER FOUR

CHARLIE had the strangest dream that night. She dreamt that Marco Delmari was making love to her. She could feel his hands on her body…his lips on her lips…demanding, ruthless yet so erotic that she woke up breathless, her heart pounding.

'Foolish in the extreme,' she berated herself as she lay looking up at the ceiling. Perhaps she had been so long without sex that her brain was turning to mush.

Karen was right, she thought. She really needed to get back out into the world of relationships again. Although she'd had a few dates since her divorce none of the men had been attractive to her. The problem was that she couldn't have sex with just anybody…she had to have feelings for a man before she could sleep with him. Consequentially the last person she had slept with was her husband four and a half years ago.

Even Karen didn't know that! The fact was that she hadn't had feelings for a man in such a long time that she had started to think maybe she would never be aroused again. And now this! It was bizarre.

Her thoughts would be better occupied thinking about what she was going to do if Karen sold her agency, she told herself firmly as she got up and reached for her dressing gown. Maybe she needed to start job-hunting for something permanent now, as there were only a few weeks left on her contract with Marco.

The phone rang next to the bed and sleepily she reached to answer it. Marco's smoothly sexy Italian tones took her by surprise.

'My apologies for ringing so early, and don't worry, I'm not cancelling our lunch—I just thought I'd catch you before I head over to the hospital to check on some patients.'

'I wasn't worried,' Charlie corrected him firmly. Really, he could be very arrogant! 'Actually I'd forgotten about lunch,' she lied swiftly. 'I thought you were the plumber, ringing to arrange a time to fix my central heating.'

'Ah, I see.' Marco laughed. He had a lovely laugh…it was just as sexy as his voice. 'It must be cold in your house. Do you want me to come earlier, see if I can warm you up?'

The question made her pulses quicken. She imagined him warming her up the way he had in her dreams last night and the thought of it made her sizzle. She pulled her dressing gown around her as if by holding it firmly across her body she could shut out the crazy images. 'No, it's OK thank you.' Her voice sounded very prim even to her own ears.

'OK, but I'm not bad at fixing things,' he continued. 'It comes from being brought up in a century-old farmhouse in Tuscany. Anyway, getting back to our arrangements for this afternoon…'

Instantly she could feel butterflies in her stomach. 'You said you wanted to discuss something about work?'

'There are a number of things I want to discuss,' he said smoothly. 'But they can wait until later. I thought we could go to the Summer House. They have an excellent menu.'

'So I've heard.' Charlie had never been to that restaurant but she knew it was one of the most exclusive in the area with sweeping views out across the River Thames.

A picture rose in her mind of somewhere formal and stiff where people were elegantly dressed. What on earth would she wear to go there? She found herself doing a mental trawl through her wardrobe and not coming up with anything very suitable.

'So I'll pick you up at twelve-thirty.'

'Marco!' She cut across him abruptly. 'Do you think we could go somewhere else?'

'Yes, of course.' Marco sounded unfazed by the request. 'We can go anywhere you would like. Have you got somewhere in mind?'

Charlie thought fast. 'There is a country pub in the next village called The Waterhouse.'

'OK, we'll eat there instead. I've got to go Charlie, see you later.'

The line went dead. Charlie replaced the receiver and realised that instead of fobbing Marco off as she had intended she had capitulated very easily.

It was just one outing…she reassured herself. Moreover Marco was probably only going to talk about work. Not much to worry about really.

Charlie had hoped that by the time Marco arrived to pick her up she would be organised and ready.

The reality was that the plumber arrived to fix her heating and held her back. So everything was done in a last-minute rush. She had just stepped into a pair of black jeans and a white blouse when Marco pulled up outside.

She looked at herself in the mirror. Her hair was tied back from her face in its usual severe style and she wondered suddenly if she should try and look different today.

On impulse she pulled the tie out, allowing the golden strands to fall around her shoulders. Then instantly she regretted it. She didn't want to look as if she was trying to be glamorous, because this wasn't a real date and anyway she knew she could never compete with the women Marco usually liked on his arm.

The shrill ring of the doorbell shattered the silence of the house. It was too late to tie it back again now!

Feeling nervous, she went down to open the front door.

And as she came face to face with Marco her heart seemed to miss a beat.

'Hi.' He smiled at her and all she could think about was how handsome he was. He was wearing casual clothes, but he looked incredible in them. Chinos, a thick cable sweater and a suede jacket that emphasised the breadth of his shoulders all added up to his look of pure, sexy Italian style. And when she met those dark eyes of his she just wanted to melt.

'I am ready, but come in while I get my bag.' She moved back and held the door for him.

'You look lovely.' He didn't take his eyes off her as he stepped into the hallway.

'Thank you.' Charlie smiled self-consciously.

'You should leave your hair like that more often. It makes you look very…alluring.' He reached out a hand and touched the golden strands, running it through his fingers like liquid silk.

The gesture was nonchalant and yet it felt like such an intimate thing to do that she was aware of her heartbeats increasing and was more than aware of the *frisson* of sensuality that suddenly sprang up between them.

She took a step away and didn't know what to say to that, she felt completely out of her depth. For the past few months she had been trying to pretend that she wasn't sexually aware of Marco and now suddenly there was no hiding from it. Now there was more awareness between them than she knew how to deal with.

Marco was just a charmer, she reminded herself firmly. It didn't mean anything.

She was glad when Jack came racing downstairs at that moment, followed at a more sedate pace by her mother.

'Marco, this is my mother, Helen, and my son, Jack,' Charlie introduced them.

'Pleased to meet you.' Marco smiled at the older woman.

'And hello, Jack.' He crouched down so that he was at eye-level with the child. 'I'm pleased to meet you too. I've heard lots about you.'

Jack smiled shyly. 'Is that red car outside yours?' he asked suddenly.

'Yes, it is.'

'Wow!' Jack's dark eyes lit up.

'So you have a passion for beautiful cars…you are like a true Italian.' Marco ruffled the child's dark hair playfully.

Charlie smiled and reached for her handbag. 'We won't be long, Mum. Thanks for looking after him.'

As it was a sunny day, Marco had the top down on his car. As they zoomed along the narrow country lanes the breeze caught Charlie's hair, whipping it around her face in wild disarray.

Marco glanced over at her as he pulled the car to a stand-still in the pub car park and watched as she tried to smooth the golden strands back into place.

'I should have tied it back,' she murmured as she caught his eye.

'I don't think so.' He seemed to look at her with deep concentration and Charlie felt herself growing hot inside. Then he reached across and brushed a strand of hair back into place. 'There—perfect again.'

The light touch of his fingers against her skin made Charlie's heart contract.

'I'm pleased you changed your mind about lunch today.'

'Well, you wanted to talk about work.' She tried to think sensibly but she felt that she was drowning in his sexy eyes.

'Yes, I did.' He gave her a teasing look. 'Amongst other things.'

'As I was saying yesterday, I do think it's important that we keep a close boundary line between work and anything personal.' Was she rambling? she wondered hazily. She was

trying so hard to be level-headed. But he seemed to be very
close to her, she could smell the tang of his cologne, warm and
evocative. She remembered how he had touched her yesterday
and a wave of longing suddenly swept through her. What would
it be like to be held in his arms, feel his hands move slowly
and intimately over her body? The sudden unbidden thought
reverberated through her, making her temperature rise dra-
matically. She tried to dismiss it but the sensual picture refused
to move from her mind.

'Actually I have a notion that, where you and I are concerned, business and pleasure could fit together very nicely.'
He murmured the words huskily, his eyes on her lips.

'I don't see how…'

Marco smiled. 'Well, as you are such a practical person and
so am I…boundaries will always be in place.' He reached and
brushed his fingers lightly down over her cheek. 'Therefore the
problem ceases to exist…don't you think?' His hand lingered
at her chin, tipping her face upwards so that he could look at
her.

The intensity of his eyes and the touch of his hand against
her skin set her heart slamming against her chest. She felt her
body tense as he moved even closer. She wanted him to kiss
her…wanted it so badly that every nerve-ending in her body
seemed to be yearning for him…and yet at the same time she
was willing herself to move away, telling herself that this situation was a mistake and that she could get badly burnt. The
trouble was that the need to risk the fire was overwhelming…

'Anyway, I think talk of work can wait until later…' he
brushed a finger across the smoothness of her lips '…whereas
this…can't.' His hands gently cupped her face as his head
lowered towards hers. The touch of his lips against hers and
the way he held her as he kissed her felt incredibly sensual and
possessive. It was no gentle kiss either, it was powerfully masterful, very dominant. Charlie's senses swam with desire and

before she could think better of it she was kissing him back with a hungry response. She was aware that his fingers moved to lace through her hair, controlling her as he thoroughly explored the sweetness of her mouth.

Charlie's emotions were all over the place as he pulled away. A part of her wanted to go back into his arms, wanted him to continue kissing her. The other part was mortified by how easily she had just capitulated to his caress, by how wantonly she had returned his kisses. *He was her boss, for heaven's sake! This could only lead to disaster.*

'What on earth are we doing?' she murmured breathlessly.

He smiled at that. 'I think it's known as enjoying ourselves,' he murmured with lazy amusement.

She felt a flare of annoyance at his casual rejoinder, but whether it was at herself for kissing him back so passionately, or him for being so nonchalant about it she wasn't sure. 'You're just a flirt, Marco…' She tried to sound dismissive but there was a revealing huskiness about her tone that she didn't like.

He smiled. 'But just for the record I really do want to discuss work with you.' He turned to get out of the car. 'Come on, let's see what the food is like in this pub of yours.'

Hurriedly she stepped out after him and tried to gather herself together. Obviously he wasn't even giving that kiss a second thought, so she needed to be as cool and urbane about it as he was. The trouble was, she couldn't think of anything cool or urbane to say.

They continued on down to the pub in silence. The Waterhouse was an old coaching house nestled in the curve of the River Thames. Behind it there was a small beer garden where people could sit on a sunny day and admire the view. Today, however, only the hardiest of souls were sitting outside in the autumn sun and it was a pleasure to walk into the warmth of the slightly dark old-world interior.

Marco stood back to allow Charlie to enter the building first and as he did so he noted the way her long hair swung silkily around her back, noted the long length of her legs, the lovely curve of her bottom in the tight-fitting jeans.

She really was quite sexy; he'd been blown away when she opened the door to him earlier, her face flushed, and her hair tumbling around her shoulders. He'd often watched her in the office and wondered what she would be like when she let her barriers down and relaxed. He had suspected that behind that prim and proper demeanour there was a hidden sensuality, and he had been right. The way she had kissed him had proved that without a doubt.

Now he found himself wanting to tear down the rest of her barriers and take her to bed.

They found a table next to a roaring log fire and Marco pulled out a chair for her to sit down. 'What can I get you to drink?'

'A glass of white wine would be nice, thank you.'

As Marco waited for the barmaid to get their drinks he glanced back at the table. Charlie was taking off her jacket now to hang it over the back of her chair. His gaze flicked over her contemplatively. Usually the women he dated were dressed in more obviously seductive apparel, yet there was something very appealing about the plain white blouse that Charlie wore. It was fitted in at her small waist and it emphasised in a subtle way the full curve of her breasts.

She glanced over and caught him watching her and he smiled before turning back to the bar.

She really was quite lovely; in fact she even brought out a protective streak in him that he hadn't felt for a while. It was something to do with the way she could look quite vulnerable at times…like just now when she'd caught him watching her…and the way she had looked at him yesterday with that defensive sparkle in her eyes as she talked about her classic love-songs CD and her parents falling in love at first sight.

He had to admit, when she had told him that she would consider a relationship that was based on realism rather than a starry-eyed premise he had been sceptical to begin with. He had already judged her and in emotional terms he had placed her in the high-maintenance bracket.

It wasn't that Marco was against the idea of love…he just didn't believe that it conquered all, and he didn't want to get involved in a relationship with someone who believed that it did. He had learnt at first hand how unrealistic expectations could tear people apart. He had watched his own parents destroy each other; it had been painful and messy and he certainly didn't want to get involved in a relationship like that. In fact he didn't really want a serious relationship in his life at all… The girls he usually went out with were fine for short-term flings, but they didn't understand his theories regarding long-term relationships at all. However, a liaison with someone of a like mind…someone who wasn't emotionally driven… well, that was a different matter.

Until yesterday he had never suspected for one moment that Charlie might be that like-minded individual. But any woman who could say she was looking for companionship had to have relegated love to a secondary position in her life. And he had realised that maybe she wasn't looking for that all-consuming love, maybe she had been hurt so much in her first marriage that she was looking now for more practical and realistic relationships.

He shouldn't have been so surprised to discover this about her but he still was—surprised and genuinely pleased because not only did it leave him free to pursue her, but it also meant that she could be quite an asset to him professionally.

The fact was that right at this moment Marco was getting very tired of giving interviews that suddenly veered off to dwell on his own personal life. It didn't seem to matter that he had produced the evidence for his theories already—people still wanted to know about his romantic circumstances. And as Sarah had pointed out, the problem wasn't going to go away. In fact when he went on his book tour to America it would probably get worse.

So having someone like Charlie around, someone who thought in the same way he did, was great. Having her in the background right now just might help play down all those annoying little questions about how his personal life compared with his theories.

The fact that he also wanted to get her into bed was simply a bonus. He hadn't planned to kiss her in the car, but the temptation had been too strong to resist and had taken him a little by surprise. As had her hungry response to him.

He returned to the table and put the drinks down.

'Thanks.' She smiled and tried not to notice that there was a group of women in the corner who were looking over at Marco with undisguised admiration.

He didn't seem to notice them at all. 'It's very pleasant in here,' he said as he took the seat opposite to her and sat with his back to them.

'Yes…kind of quaint…' She took a sip of her drink.

'So how do you usually spend your Saturdays?' he asked suddenly.

'Mostly my weekends are taken up by spending time with Jack and catching up on housework.' She shrugged. 'I'm sure your weekends are very different!'

'It must be difficult working full-time and looking after a house and a child.'

'Sometimes, but I have a child-minder and good back-up from my mother. My dad died a few years ago so in a way Jack has been company for Mum, and helped focus her attention away from her grief.'

'It's good to have family support.'

Charlie nodded. 'But I try not to put on Mum too much. She

has a busy life. That's why I decided to work for a temping agency; it's been great while Jack's been small because it's given me flexibility.' Charlie raked a hand through her hair. It looked as though all that was going to finish if Karen sold the agency, she thought distractedly.

'And Jack's dad doesn't help out at all in this arrangement?'

Charlie focused on him again and shook her head. 'Greg is a pilot and he is based in America now, he has an apartment in LA.'

'He doesn't see his son at all?'

Charlie could hear the note of disbelief in Marco's voice. 'Greg's life is busy. And, although he does fly into London, he's on a tight turn-around schedule—well, that's the excuse I give Jack, anyway.'

'I see.'

As she met his steady gaze Charlie wondered if Marco was thinking how reprehensible it was for her to lie about why Jack's father didn't see him.

She knew Greg would actually have plenty of time to see his son in between flying around the world. But how could you tell a four-year-old that his father wasn't interested in him?

Marco looked at the bright blaze in her eyes as she looked across at him, and noticed the way she raised her chin slightly. Obviously the mere mention of Jack's father still had the power to touch Charlie on an emotional level.

'Anyway, enough about that.' She changed the subject swiftly. 'You wanted to talk about work, not listen to me rambling on…'

Marco noticed that once more the shutters had come down over her expression. 'You weren't rambling on and I was interested,' he said softly. 'Your ex still has the power to upset you, doesn't he?'

She didn't like the observation. 'What makes you think that?'

'I don't know…it could be something to do with the expression in your eyes whenever he's mentioned.'

'I'm not upset about Greg.' There was a hint of steel in her tone suddenly. 'I'm just upset for Jack. I feel for him and the fact that he doesn't see his dad.'

'That's understandable.'

'Well, that's all it is. Apart from the fact that I have his son, Greg is history.' She angled her chin up even more. 'So…let's get back to why we are here. You wanted to discuss work.'

Marco hesitated. He wanted to delve deeper, but if he wanted to get closer to her he was going to have to break down her defences and get her to open up to him. Maybe now wasn't the time.

He drummed his fingers on the table for a moment before making a decision. For now he would drop the personal questions and concentrate on things from the safety zone of work. He was going to have to take things slowly.

'OK…' Marco looked up and fixed her with a dark, penetrating look that made her insides tighten '…as you know, your contract with me is coming to an end soon. But I'd like you to consider extending it, staying on.'

She hadn't been expecting this! 'How long were you thinking?' she asked swiftly.

Marco shrugged. 'Another twelve months, possibly longer, we'll see how we go from there.'

Charlie felt a dart of pleasure mixed with relief. 'That would be great.' She smiled at him. 'To be honest, the offer couldn't have come at a better time. I think the agency I work for will be sold soon and I was wondering what I should do after that.'

'It will suit us both, then.' Marco sat back in his chair, feeling pleased. He had been planning to offer Charlie a permanent job regardless of his personal interest in her. He really didn't want to lose her from the office. Things had never run as smoothly as they did now. The added advantage that this would make it easier to get closer made the agreement very sweet. 'Shall we say the same hours?' he said nonchalantly. 'I know it's not easy working full-time having a young child, but I can be flexible.'

'Thanks, I'd appreciate that.' She looked over at him gratefully. 'It can be a nightmare sometimes if Jack's ill.'

'I understand.' Marco nodded. 'The only thing is I'll need you to accompany me on a few trips now and then, seminars...that kind of thing.'

Charlie hesitated before answering him, and he could see her weighing up the fact that she didn't want to leave her child alongside the fact that she wanted this job.

'It will be mainly over the next few months but after that things should settle back to normal,' Marco told her gently.

She nodded. 'Well, it shouldn't be a problem, then.'

'Great. As you know, I've got a very busy period coming up with this book tour so I'm delighted to sort that out.'

She smiled at him, feeling a surge of happiness. Twelve months working with Marco sounded like bliss. She really did like him, Charlie thought suddenly. Maybe she even liked him too much. The thought distracted her from what he was saying, and her gaze started to drift over the rugged, handsome contours of his features. She found herself lingering for a moment on his lips as she remembered how sensational his kiss had been.

'So you are OK with all of that?' He fixed her with that intently sexy look of his and she felt her heart starting to slam against her chest again.

Was she OK with all of this? The exuberant feeling of relief she had experienced when he'd asked her to stay on began to fade a little. How was she going to maintain a professional relationship with a man who made her feel like this?

'Charlie?'

Aware that he was waiting for an answer, she quickly pulled herself together. She had a pile of bills waiting on the sideboard and a house that desperately needed even more money spent on it. According to the plumber this morning, she was probably going to need a whole new central-heating system. She couldn't afford to allow irrational feelings to mess up a job opportunity.

'Yes, perfectly.'

'Good.' He smiled at her and for a moment his eyes drifted lazily over her. 'Well, now the main business is out of the way, we should relax and order something to eat.'

Charlie picked up the menu from the table. Relaxing around Marco was probably not a good idea, because that was when these feelings of attraction started to strike. Things would be OK once they got back into the office, she reassured herself firmly. They were always so busy; there would be no time for anything personal.

'I have to go to Tuscany at the weekend,' Marco said suddenly.

'Oh?' She looked over at him with interest. 'You were telling me on the phone that you grew up there. What was it you said—a century-old farmhouse? It sounded lovely.'

'Yes, it is. Have you ever been to Italy?'

Charlie shook her head.

'Well, the villa is set in a very beautiful area. In the summer the meadows are alight with the gold of sunflowers…just hectare after hectare of them under a blazing blue sky. And right now there will be a mellow warmth in the air and they will be harvesting the vines.'

'How did you ever bear to leave a place as beautiful as that?'

'Very easily actually.' He smiled ruefully. 'I'm not the sentimental type.'

'Of course.' Charlie forgot herself for a moment and looked at him teasingly. 'Because that could go under the heading of being romantic…and you wouldn't want that.'

'Definitely not.' Marco smiled.

As their eyes met that feeling of awareness and intimacy

suddenly sprang forcefully to life between them again. Charlie could feel it twisting in the air like a living entity ready to coil around her and draw her deeper and deeper under its spell.

Desperately she tried to ignore it. 'So are your parents still at the farmhouse?' She moved the conversation on.

'Unfortunately my parents died in a car crash five years ago.'

'I'm so sorry, Marco. That's awful!'

'Yes.' He met her eyes candidly. 'I've come to terms with it now. But it was a traumatic time.'

She nodded.

'I still own the farmhouse and sometimes my sisters bring their children there for holidays, but apart from that the place lies empty.'

'That's a shame.'

'I suppose it is.' Marco shrugged. 'Anyway, I'll be there for the weekend. It's a business trip but it will give me the opportunity to check on the place. And the reason I've mentioned it is that, now you have agreed to work for me permanently, I want you to accompany me.'

The invitation was tagged on so casually that Charlie wasn't sure how to take it. She looked across at him and her heart started its rapid tattoo again. 'You mean on business, of course?'

'Of course.'

Charlie cringed and wished now she hadn't sought clarification!

'There will be time for us to get to know each other along more personal lines as well,' he added softly.

As their eyes met her emotions seemed to race with peculiar intensity, pleasure…panic and a large helping of desire all seemed to merge and flutter. A weekend in romantic Tuscany getting to know Marco Delmari would probably be better than all her wildest fantasies put together.

Stop it, Charlie, she warned herself furiously. *This is dangerous territory.*

Marco watched the uncertainty chasing across the shadows of her green eyes and smiled. 'I was thinking a trip to Florence and dinner,' he said teasingly. 'Sharing a bedroom is optional.'

The provocative words made her skin flare a bright crimson. 'You know, Marco, I think you like to make outrageous statements just to ruffle my equilibrium and get a rise out of me.' With difficulty she kept her tone light.

She noticed the gleam in his dark eyes. 'You're probably right,' he said. 'You do look very attractive when you blush. And it's such a rare attribute these days.'

Charlie tried as hard as she could to remain impassive to that remark. She was damned if she was going to give him the satisfaction of getting another response. 'Just for the record, I wasn't worried about the sleeping arrangements.'

'Good.' He smiled at her and she felt her insides starting to heat up again.

And that was when she knew for certain that she was lying. The knowledge curled uncomfortably inside her.

She wasn't worried that Marco would pressurise her into sleeping with him—she knew instinctively he wasn't that kind of man. Apart from anything else, there was any number of women who would willingly do that. And, despite the way he had kissed her and his teasing comments, she was sure Marco's priorities where she was concerned were mainly businesslike. The only thing that had changed between them was that he now believed she was on his wavelength emotionally, which meant he viewed her as fair game for a casual fling...

What concerned her were her reactions to him. The way she had found herself responding to his kisses scared her a little. She hadn't been turned on like that in such a long time and now she wondered what would happen if he touched her or kissed her when they were alone together in Italy.

Would she be able to pull back from the situation?

She felt a swirl of deep anxiety. If anything happened

between her and Marco and things went wrong she could ultimately lose her job. Going away with him could be a big mistake.

But how could she avoid it? She bit down on her lip and tried to think sensibly. This was business…and Marco had made it clear that he expected her to accompany him on a few trips. It was hardly an unreasonable request, given the salary he was paying. And. although it was fairly short notice, she knew her mother would be only too happy to have her grandson with her for a whole weekend.

'So what exactly is involved work-wise?' she asked cautiously.

'It's fairly straightforward.' He shrugged. 'I'm giving an interview for Italian TV to promote my book. That will take up a lot of time on Sunday and I have a stack of notes in my office at the villa that need to be catalogued ready for a meeting later that evening back in London with Professor Hunt.'

It sounded reasonable enough. And if she couldn't handle her emotions around him she was going to mess this opportunity up before it started. 'Fine,' she said calmly. 'It's only one weekend it shouldn't be a problem.'

Was it her imagination or was there a gleam of triumph in his dark gaze now?

Charlie hurriedly dismissed the thought. This was business and she needed the job.

CHAPTER FIVE

WHAT was she doing, Charlie wondered in agitation as the fasten-seatbelt sign came on and the pilot told them to prepare for landing. She should never have agreed to this…it was madness!

As she looked up her eyes connected with Marco's. 'Not long now and we'll be on the ground.'

Charlie forced herself to smile at him.

The sudden panic had hit her mid-flight out of nowhere, which was strange because during the week she had managed to convince herself that she wasn't in the slightest bit concerned about this trip. She supposed the fact that it had been extremely busy in the office had helped.

Marco had been his usual friendly self but the familiarity that had flared over last weekend had seemingly been forgotten. In fact as soon as he had dropped her off at home after lunch last Saturday it had been forgotten, although maybe not entirely by her. Sometimes when she had glanced up and caught his eye the memory of that kiss had been there, but it had been a fleeting thing and it hadn't encroached on work.

But now, sitting next to him on the plane, she felt all those dangerous feelings of desire flooding back in force. Suddenly she was aware of everything about him. The scent of his cologne, even the way his arm brushed lightly against hers as he moved made her tingle with consciousness.

It was only because they were out of their usual environment, she told herself soothingly. As soon as they started to work at his office in the villa things would be fine again, common sense would snap back into place and these silly feelings would go.

'You've forgotten to fasten your seat belt,' Marco reminded her.

She made to reach for it, but he had already found it and was leaning across to slip it into place.

For a second he was so close that she could feel the strength of his hard-muscled arms through the light material of her blouse. She tensed at the fleeting touch of his hands against her waist, her senses pounding.

'There.' He smiled at her and her gaze drifted from his intensely sexy eyes to the firm, sensual curve of his lips.

'Better safe than sorry—isn't that what they say?' he said lightly as he sat back.

That saying should be branded on her consciousness for the entire weekend, Charlie thought wryly, because if she didn't get a grip she was going to be in deep water.

'Thanks.' She smiled politely and then turned to look out of the window into the darkness of the night.

She hoped he didn't know what kind of an effect he was having on her because that would be too embarrassing. He would be totally amused.

A picture of the kind of amusement he could find flicked through her mind in a searing, red-hot vision of them entwined in a double bed.

Stop it, Charlie! If you value your job you won't even think about that.

She clenched her hands at her sides and reminded herself in severe terms of just how important this job was. Karen was in the process of selling the agency...they had talked a few days ago and it seemed the deal would go through pretty quickly.

If she didn't stay on with Marco she could be in financial limbo for a while. She had no doubt that she would find another job but it could take time and she would be lucky to find something as well-paid.

The plane touched down and there was a screech of brakes.

Don't let yourself think about anything that isn't related to business, she told herself briskly. It was Friday night now, and their flight home was booked for late Sunday afternoon. All she had to do was hold her nerve and keep her distance for two short days.

As the plane came to a halt Marco stood up and collected the hand luggage from the overhead compartment.

He put an arm around her as they stepped out into the mellow warmth of the night air. 'Welcome to Italy…' He murmured the words against her ear, making her senses sizzle.

It didn't mean anything…he was just being Italian, she assured herself. But even so, it was enough to bring her panic racing back. Yes, it was only two days *and two nights…with Marco*…a man who could turn her on with a mere whisper.

'Thanks…' She tried very hard to sound businesslike. 'Maybe one day I'll come here for pleasure rather than business.'

'I think we can make some time for pleasure,' Marco said with amusement.

Would sharing a bed come under that remit? she wondered suddenly. The question pulsated through her along with the touch of his hand and the knowledge that she was aching to be even closer!

With difficulty she broke the contact and stepped away from him. 'Well, we'll see. But we have a lot of work to do,' she said briskly.

He smiled. 'I knew we would make a good team. With you by my side I need never fall behind with work again.'

She wasn't sure if he was being facetious or serious. There

was a gleam in his eye that was very disconcerting. 'I'd better go collect my luggage…'

Marco watched her walk away, a look of contemplation in his eyes. She was as jumpy as a skittish colt. This weekend in Italy was just what they needed. He would break through her barriers, he told himself firmly. He was determined about that. When he wanted something he usually got it.

Marco didn't have any luggage to collect, as everything he needed was already at the villa, so he went to see about their hire car while Charlie waited by the carousel for her case.

They met in the arrivals hall a little while later, and within a few minutes Charlie was installed in the passenger seat of a Mercedes and they were heading away from the town of Pisa into the countryside.

Charlie switched on her mobile phone and checked to see if there were any messages from her mother. There was nothing, which probably meant that everything was fine and Jack was in bed.

Marco glanced over and noticed the phone. 'Are you going to give Jack a ring?'

'He goes to bed at seven-thirty, so he'll be asleep now. I like to keep him in a routine.'

Marco nodded. 'Kids like routine. It makes them feel safe.'

Routine could also make adults feel safe, Charlie thought as she watched the powerful headlights slicing through the darkness of the narrow lanes. Usually at this time on a Friday after she had read Jack his bedtime story and tucked him in, she would catch up on chores around the house before settling down to watch TV. If she was honest she had to admit that she had been hiding away behind her routine for the last few years. She had preferred it and she hadn't wanted a relationship. The bottom line was, if you didn't open up to people then you didn't get hurt. But, as Karen said, she couldn't hide forever and it was time she started dating again.

But not with Marco, she reminded herself firmly. She needed this job too badly to risk any involvement with him…he was out of bounds.

'This is the first time I've left him overnight.' She snapped her phone closed again.

'It must feel a bit strange, then.'

'Yes…a bit.' She smiled over at him. 'Although not quite as strange as dropping him off at school for the first time at the beginning of this month, he looked so grown-up in his uniform.'

'At least he likes school. My sister's youngest child cried every morning when she was dropped off. It broke Julia's heart.'

'How distressing for her.' Charlie glanced over at him curiously. 'Where does your sister live?'

'Julia is in Ireland. She's married and has four children. My sister Tess is in France working as an interpreter for a law firm. Then my sister Maggie lives in Norway with her partner and they have three children.'

'How lovely to have sisters. Have you any brothers?'

'No, there was just me.' He grinned. 'I'm the eldest. The one who bosses them around.'

'And looks out for them,' Charlie guessed. She had heard the warmth in his tone. 'It must be nice to be part of a big family,' she said wistfully.

'You don't have any siblings?'

'No, I was an only child.' She glanced over at him curiously. 'So what was it like growing up in a predominantly female household?'

'Put it this way, I was very glad when we had some *en suites* fitted, because before that I seemed to spend years queuing outside bathroom doors.'

Charlie laughed.

'That's better.' Marco glanced over at her and smiled. 'You seem more relaxed now. You were a bit tense earlier.'

'Was I?' Charlie cringed; she'd hoped he hadn't noticed! 'Sorry I was a bit distracted.'

He looked over at her questioningly.

'Thinking about the office…' she improvised hastily.

'Really?' His voice was dry. He didn't sound as if he believed her.

He flicked an amused glance over at her and she felt herself blush. It did sound unbelievable that she would be thinking about the office on a Friday evening in Tuscany!

Marco smiled. 'Do you want to know what I was thinking?'

She *really* hoped he wasn't going to make some glib comment that would make her embarrassed. It would be just like him to tease her about the sleeping arrangements right now.

'I was wondering if we should stop off at a little *trattoria* I know for something to eat or if we should head straight to the villa and I'll cook.'

'Oh!' She relaxed and smiled.

'You know, I've never met anyone who thought about work more than me.' He continued on in a jovial tone, 'It's a whole new experience.'

'Well, you know what they say,' she said lightly; 'if something is worth doing, it's worth doing well… So, getting back to your thoughts…' swiftly she changed the subject, '…can you cook?'

'Of course; why do you sound so surprised?'

'Maybe because you are always so immersed in work I didn't think you'd have time to spend in the kitchen.'

'Oh, I make time for food.' Marco laughed. 'After all, I'm Italian. Food is one of our passions.'

Charlie smiled and tried not to allow her mind to race towards what his other passions might be.

Marco paused the car at a junction. 'So, are we eating out tonight or shall I cook for us?'

Somehow whatever option she chose sounded perilously cosy! 'When do you want to get down to doing some work?' she countered instead.

'You've already got the job, Charlie; you don't need to try and impress me with your dedication a moment longer.' He grinned.

'I wasn't trying to impress you, I was being—'

'Practical,' he finished for her wryly. 'And I really like that about you. But you know what, Charlie? Let's give practicality a rest for now. It is Friday night. We can think about the office tomorrow.'

'Fine…'

What else could she say? Charlie wondered frantically.

'Tell you what, I'll cook…it will give us a chance to talk without being interrupted. We can go out tomorrow.' The decision made, Marco put the car into gear again and moved away from the junction.

Talk about what? It was all sounding a little too intimate for her peace of mind Charlie thought warily. 'Well, maybe that's best,' she murmured. 'After all, we are both a bit tired and we might want an early night.' She made the statement thinking it might be a good escape route for later, but as soon as the words were out she realised they sounded riskily provocative.

'We might indeed.' He smiled at her and as their eyes met she felt a tug of sexual attraction that was so fierce it was almost palpable.

Hurriedly she looked away. 'So, do we need to stop off and get some groceries?'

'No, Rita, my housekeeper, will have done all that.'

Her spirits lifted a little. Maybe they wouldn't be entirely alone after all. 'I didn't realise you had a housekeeper. Does she live in?'

'No, but she will have done the shopping, made up the bed and the fires will be lit. So the place should be aired and warm.'

He'd said *bed*, she noticed. Shouldn't he have said *beds?* Maybe it was just a slip of the tongue…maybe it was his accent and he had said beds but she hadn't heard him correctly. Or maybe he was taking it for granted that she would fall into his arms and his bed. Let's face it, she thought, there couldn't be many women who would turn him down…

Don't even think about it, Charlie, she told herself heatedly.

The road was winding up out of the valley now. Charlie could see the dark shapes of cypress trees against the clear midnight-blue of the sky. A few houses were dotted along the way, throwing golden light into the lonely darkness.

Marco turned the car up into a driveway, gravel crunching beneath the tyres as they drove higher then rounded a corner and came to a halt in front of a large stone building.

'Here we are.' He switched the engine off and they both stepped out of the car. They were high up and probably by day there was a spectacular view out over the valley, but all she could see was the clearness of the night sky ablaze with stars against the shadowy darkness of the landscape. There was silence except for the sound of cicadas and the air was fragrant with blossom.

Marco handed Charlie the keys of the front door. 'You open up and I'll get your case.'

The front door opened into a large flagged hallway. There was a vase of fresh lilies on the table and their perfume filled the air. Through an open doorway Charlie could see a lounge with a stone fireplace at one end where a log fire was blazing. A few lamps had been left on, throwing a subdued glow over the polished maple floor and the white furniture.

Marco came in behind her.

'Your house is lovely.'

'Thanks. Come on, I'll show you upstairs.'

As he led the way up the curving staircase Charlie tried not to think about how intimate this was. They turned onto the landing and Marco opened up a door then stood back to allow her to enter the room first.

The first thing she noticed was the huge double bed, its crisp white covers folded back invitingly. A log fire crackled inside a wood-burning stove and there were some pine logs and cones in a basket beside it, which probably accounted for the fresh scent in the room.

'This is lovely. Thank you.' She watched as he put down her case. Then he straightened and looked over at her.

They were standing inches apart and for a while there was silence between them, the only sound the crackle of the fire and the drum of her heartbeat.

He really was far too handsome for any woman's peace of mind, she thought distractedly. She wanted to take a step backwards from him…and at the same time perversely she wanted to reach out and run her hands up and along the broad contours of his shoulders, until her fingers found the dark thickness of his hair.

Marco watched the way she put her hands behind her back and stepped away, and noted the guarded expression in her green eyes.

'In case you are wondering, I've given you the room directly across the corridor from mine.'

'Oh…I wasn't wondering,' she said lightly.

He smiled and she could tell he knew she was lying.

'Of course, you don't necessarily need to stay in here.' There was that teasing sound in his deep voice again. 'There are six bedrooms along this landing. You can have any one of them you want.'

'I'll bear that in mind.'

Marco was watching her as if she was the most entertaining of creatures. 'Well, now we have that sorted out I'll go and get dinner underway. I'll see you downstairs when you are ready.'

'Thanks.'

As soon as the door closed behind him Charlie sank down onto the bed. He obviously just enjoyed bantering with her but she felt so emotionally drained it was as if it had taken every last ounce of strength just to keep the situation light and keep her distance from him.

Across the room she caught a glimpse of her reflection in the cheval mirror. She had travelled in jeans and a blue silk blouse and her hair was tied back from her face in the usual style she wore for work. She looked smartly casual but nowhere near as glamorous as the women Marco dated.

For all his teasing remarks, he wasn't really interested in her, she reminded herself. She wasn't his type. Of course, the fact that he now believed she was in tune with his theories on romance meant he was more interested in her than he had been before. And no doubt, given any encouragement, he would sleep with her…but it would just be light entertainment to him, something to fill a gap.

Knowing all these things as she did, why was she having such difficulty switching off her feelings of attraction for him? It made her angry. She had promised herself when Greg left her that no man would ever take her for a fool again. So why was she even tempted to play with fire now?

With renewed vigour she stood up and opened her case to take out a change of clothing. She wasn't going to allow stupid feelings of a short-lived desire to ruin her working relationship with Marco. She would have dinner with him and she would laugh and joke with him but *she would keep him at arm's length.*

Twenty minutes later she went back downstairs, her mood focused and determined.

She found Marco in the kitchen at the back of the house.

He turned as she walked in and his gaze moved slowly over her, taking in the black dress cinched in at her small waist with a wide leather belt, before moving down to her high-heeled suede boots.

Charlie tried very hard not to allow her new-found self-assurance slip. There was something very Italian about the way he didn't try to hide the fact that he was looking at her with purely sexual interest.

'You look great,' he said softly. 'And I know I've said it before but you should wear your hair loose like that all the time.'

'It would get in the way at work.'

'It might.' He nodded, a spark of devilment in his dark eyes now. 'But not for the reasons you mean.'

The warmth of his tone made her pulses quicken, made her very aware of the flare of attraction between them. Their eyes held each other's gaze for a moment too long…before she quickly pulled her senses together.

'Do you need any help with dinner?'

He smiled as he noted how abruptly she changed the subject. 'No; everything is under control. Take a seat.' He nodded towards one of the high stools at the breakfast bar. 'I'll pour you a glass of wine.'

'Thanks.' She did as he asked and watched as he uncorked a bottle of red.

'This comes from the vineyard next door.'

Charlie took the glass he offered and tasted the drink; it had rich, fruity undertones. 'I'm not a connoisseur by any means but this is very good.'

'Most of the Italian wines are,' he said matter-of-factly.

'Not that you are biased or anything,' she added with a smile.

'Heavens, no! Whatever gave you that idea?'

She grinned and raised her glass towards his. 'Here's to Italy,' she said.

He touched his glass against hers. 'No, here's to your first visit to Italy. May it be the first of many.'

Charlie tried not to be distracted by the warmth of those words. Her gaze moved from him towards the rustic charm of the kitchen with its maple cupboards and dark flagged floors. There was an enormous wine rack at one side, completely full of bottles. 'Were your family in the wine-making business as well?'

'No, my grandfather grew flowers, hence the name…La Casa del Fiori…house of flowers.'

'If you don't mind my saying, that sounds very romantic.' Charlie looked over at him mischievously and he laughed.

'It might sound that way, but I assure you it wasn't. The flowers were grown for purely commercial purposes. When my grandfather died he left the place to my father and we moved here from Milan. My father was an architect so the flower business was not to his liking. He rented the land off and worked in the town near-by.'

Charlie watched as he chopped some herbs. He looked totally at home in this kitchen and more relaxed than she had ever seen him. She noticed that he had changed out of the clothes he had travelled in and was now wearing a chunky black sweater teamed with a pair of black jeans. His hair gleamed dark under the overhead light.

'Do you feel as if you've come home when you come here?' she asked curiously.

'Not really. This hasn't been my home for a very long time. After I left to go to university I didn't come back here….except for visits, of course.'

'And you haven't been tempted to sell it?'

'The thought has crossed my mind, but it's been in the family for generations; I just couldn't bring myself to do it.'

'So it must hold happy memories for you.'

'Some…' Marco shrugged. 'But in truth this house never rang with much happiness. My mother hated it, she was a city person, born and brought up in Milan. To her the countryside was great for a day out, nothing more…she felt trapped here.'

'And yet it is so beautiful.'

'You can get used to beautiful scenery…and so bored after a while that you don't even notice it any more.'

'I can't imagine ever being that bored,' Charlie murmured. 'It sounds sad.'

'Yes, I suppose it is.' Marco looked over at her contemplatively. 'But unfortunately one man's paradise can be another's prison. There has to be more substance to a situation than just what you can see. My father was a countryman at heart and he couldn't understand why my mother wouldn't settle here. He thought that if she loved him she would be happy.'

'But love wasn't enough to keep her happy?' Charlie guessed wryly.

'That's about it in a nutshell. I think my father would have moved back to Milan for her, but unfortunately by the time he realised just how much she hated this place his finances were already tied up. He had bought into a business partnership and it's not so easy to walk away from your own business, even if you want to.'

'So what happened—did the marriage end in divorce?'

'No, my father didn't believe in divorce. My mother got herself a job in Milan and lived most of the time there under the guise of work…then came home at weekends. We all knew she had another man in her life but it was never spoken about.'

Charlie looked over at him with sympathy. 'That must have been a difficult situation for everyone.'

'It wasn't a picnic.'

Charlie sensed that the flippant reply hid a rawness that probably was still with him to this day.

'Do you think your belief that love isn't enough to sustain a relationship stems from what happened between your parents?' She asked the question impulsively.

Marco looked over at her and laughed. 'Are you trying to analyse me, Charlie?'

'Maybe.' She blushed a little.

'Well, I don't think I'm particularly scarred by what happened, but when you watch two people you love destroy each other I suppose it has an effect. And we are all products of our past.' One sardonic eyebrow lifted as he fixed her with that probing look of his.

'Yes, I suppose we are.'

'So now we've discussed my hang-ups, shall we have a turn at dissecting yours?'

For some reason the quietly asked question hit on a sensitive nerve. 'I don't have any hang-ups.'

Suddenly his eyes were completely serious. 'What about those great steel barriers that come down as soon as anyone starts to try and get close to you?'

'I don't know what you are talking about,' she said quickly.

The expression in Marco's eyes was so intensely perceptive that she found herself dropping her gaze. 'So...is dinner nearly ready, because I don't mind telling you that I'm ravenous?'

For a moment she thought he wasn't going to let her move the subject so easily, but after a brief pause, he went along with her. 'Yes, antipasti is ready to be served,' he said light-heartedly, 'so if you will follow me through to the dining room...'

He moved to open a sliding door beside him and Charlie found herself looking through into a dining room where a table was laid for two.

The setting was one of seduction. A table was laid with white linen and silverware, and there were candles flickering along the sideboard and on the table, reflecting over polished surfaces.

'All Rita's handiwork,' Marco admitted as he saw her look of surprise. 'She always has everything perfect for me.'

'I see.' As Charlie moved further into the room she felt a flare of annoyance mixed with trepidation. Obviously Rita was well-used to him bringing his conquests here. 'You forgot to tell your housekeeper that I'm just your employee, not your girlfriend.'

'I haven't forgotten anything, Charlie,' he said quietly. He caught hold of her arm as she made to move past him. 'We both know that there is a connection between us that is deeper than that…'

As she looked up at him the memory of their kiss swirled inside her with vivid intensity. She pushed it back with difficulty. *It meant nothing.* 'You mean the fact that we both view romance with a sceptical eye?'

'I view romance with a rational eye,' he corrected her firmly. 'And I was talking about the fact that we've been drawn to each other recently but we've been sidestepping the feeling.'

'I haven't noticed anything.' The lie dropped quickly from her lips.

'Of course you have. You know it and I know it.' His hand moved to touch her cheek; it was the lightest of caresses yet it burnt against her senses like an iron brand.

And suddenly her breath felt as if it was painful to draw. She wanted him to kiss her again…wanted him so badly it hurt. The knowledge terrified her.

'Marco, don't.' Her voice was filled with a sudden panic.

'Don't what?'

Her eyes seemed too large for her small face. Marco saw the way they clouded with desire, but he also noted the way she almost flinched away from him.

'Don't assume that I am just another one of your conquests, because I'm not,' she told him angrily. 'It doesn't matter how many candles you light or how many lies you generate—'

'Charlie!' he cut across her firmly. 'I wasn't thinking of telling you any lies.' He sounded mildly surprised by the accusation. 'Generally speaking, I think I'm an honest person. And believe it or not I wanted to spend time getting to know you this evening because I like you…' He looked at her pointedly. 'I know you find that hard to believe but it's true.'

The gentle sincerity in his tone totally disarmed her for a second.

'And I have no intention of pouncing on you,' he added. 'It's not my style.'

'I know that,' she said swiftly.

'Well, at least that's something.' He raked a hand through the thick darkness of his hair. 'Because the way you flinched a moment ago, I was concerned that was what you were thinking.'

'Of course not!' She felt guilty now! Her fear had been directed inwardly at her own reactions towards him…never the other way round. 'Look, I don't know why I said those things,' she admitted huskily. 'I just felt a bit…'

'Tense?' He supplied the word with a mocking smile. 'Yes, I have noticed.'

Feeling acutely embarrassed, Charlie moved to sit down at the table. 'I'm just worried we will mess up our working relationship,' she said lightly.

'That is only part of what is bothering you.' Marco pulled up a chair and sat down beside her. 'This goes deeper than just being worried about your job.'

She stared at him for a moment, her heart thundering against her chest. Of course, he was right. This did go deeper. Yes, she was concerned about her work…she really needed this job. But there was more to her fears than that.

'I think the truth is something much closer to your heart—'

'Just leave it, Marco,' she warned him unsteadily.

He ignored her. 'I think you've been hurt so badly in the past that you tend to run in the opposite direction from any emotional contact.'

When she didn't answer him immediately he reached out a

hand and brushed her hair back from her face so that he could see her expression. The gesture was tenderly provocative and it was that rather than his words that caused the feelings which had been locked away deep inside her to reverberate with violent force.

She looked up and met his eyes.

'I'm right, aren't I?'

'Maybe…' She admitted the truth huskily. The touch of his hand against her skin sent little shivers of need racing through her.

He let his hand drop and sat back with a smile. 'So now that we are being completely honest with each other…no barriers whatsoever, I do have a confession to make too.'

'What's that?' She looked over at him with a frown.

'The idea of trying to get you into my bed has crossed my mind…' He spread his hands and looked at her with a glint of devilment in his dark eyes. 'Of course it has…what can I say…? I'm Italian…a red-blooded male. And I find you attractive.'

'You are also my boss, which makes it a conflict of interest.' She found the strength to rally herself from the feelings of desire that were flooding through her in mutinous waves.

'Maybe.' He shrugged. 'But why don't we forget about conflicts of interest for one evening? In fact, why don't we forget about everything, put all our preconceived ideas about each other to one side, and just enjoy having dinner together and getting to know each other?'

When she didn't answer him immediately he smiled.

'Or does that sound a little too dangerous?'

The challenge in that question sounded so absurd that Charlie laughed. 'No, it doesn't sound dangerous.'

'Good. Then that is what we will do.'

Charlie met his gaze and felt a flow of warmth around the frozen loneliness of a heart she had been trying so fiercely to protect.

Where was the harm in relaxing and enjoying herself with a man she felt attracted to?

She leaned back in her chair and smiled at him, his soothing words obscuring the fear that she had just made a fatal mistake by lowering her defences.

CHAPTER SIX

To say that Marco was a charismatic dinner companion was putting it mildly. She couldn't remember a more enjoyable evening.

When she thought about it later she realised they hadn't really talked about anything of particular depth over the meal, just amusing anecdotes from their past. But Marco was incredibly funny. He made her laugh and he held her enthralled with his stories…he also listened as if he was interested in every last detail of what she had to say.

It was a long time since anyone had made her feel the way he did—as if she was the most interesting and the most beautiful woman in the world. Of course, she realised this was probably the effect he had on every woman he spent time with. She wasn't naïve enough to believe otherwise…but it was so nice to relax with him. She hadn't realised until now how much she had missed male company…how much she had missed just being herself around someone who made her feel special.

'That was a fabulous meal,' Charlie said honestly as he got up to clear the table. 'You're a great cook.'

'Comes with living on my own for so long,' he said with a shrug. 'When you've no one to share the domestic chores with it makes you sharper.'

'Well, I've been on my own for a number of years now and my domestic skills haven't improved to that standard.'

Marco went over to the sideboard and poured them both a coffee. 'How long have you been on your own?' he asked over his shoulder.

'Four and a half years.'

'That long!' He returned to the table and put the cup and saucer down in front of her with a frown. 'But Jack is only four!'

'Greg left when I was pregnant.'

Charlie's matter-of-fact tone didn't fool Marco for a moment.

'That must have been difficult to cope with,' he reflected quietly.

'It wasn't easy. I had to deal with my father's death, my pregnancy, a divorce and finding somewhere to live all at the same time.'

'Couldn't you have stayed in the house you had?'

She shook her head. 'We'd sold it already to find something more child-friendly.'

'And then your husband left before you could make the next purchase?'

She heard the distaste in his voice.

'He'd met someone else.' She shrugged. 'Anyway, I don't know why I just told you all that. I coped without him, so it doesn't matter now.'

No wonder he sometimes glimpsed that look of distrust in her eyes…that raw vulnerability. 'I'm glad you did tell me.' He put his other hand over hers and squeezed it gently. 'It makes me admire you all the more.'

'You admire me?' For a moment amusement chased the shadows in her eyes away.

She had such expressive eyes, he thought. And, despite everything, laughter came so easily to them.

'Well, yes, I do. I admire the way you've coped so well on

your own; I admire the fact that you have a great spirit. You are quite remarkable.'

Charlie laughed. 'And, of course, indispensable in the office.'

'Goes without saying.' He smiled, enjoying the sparkle of fun that danced between them.

She glanced down at his hand, so large against hers, and was aware that what had started out as a gesture of sympathy had changed into something else.

His fingers caressed slowly over her skin, and the touch was intoxicating; it sent shivers of desire racing through her in delicious little waves. Like a taster of the pleasure he could bring her given full reign.

As soon as the thought flicked through her mind she forced herself to pull away from him. That was exactly what she shouldn't be thinking about, she told herself firmly!

'I suppose we should call it a night,' she said briskly. 'We've got to get to work in the morning.'

'It shouldn't take too long with both of us going through the files.' If he noticed how abruptly she withdrew from him Marco didn't show it. 'But I suppose you are right—we should turn in.'

Charlie watched as he blew out the candles on the table and perversely she felt a stab of disappointment that the warmth that had enveloped them all evening had to come to an end.

She was being silly, she told herself. It had been a lovely evening but it was time for them to say goodnight. Otherwise… She looked over and met the darkness of his eyes and her senses wavered alarmingly. *Otherwise things could get complicated.*

Hurriedly she reached to pick up the coffee cups. 'I'll help you clear away the last of the dishes.'

'Leave everything, Charlie. I'll see to it.'

'No, honestly, it's the least I can do after you've gone to so much trouble.' She headed into the kitchen and put the crockery in the sink.

'Charlie?' His voice was very close behind her.

He put a hand on her shoulder, turning her around to face him. They were just inches apart.

'Everything in the kitchen is under control,' he said softly.

Not everything, she thought wryly. For one thing, her emotions were pounding in a way she had no control over at all.

'I've really enjoyed this evening.' His eyes moved over her with a deep contemplation that made her burn inside.

'Yes, me too,' she murmured huskily.

Charlie noticed his eyes were on her lips and she felt her heart bounce crazily against her chest. She really wanted him to kiss her. What harm would it do to have one goodnight kiss? a little voice was whispering provocatively inside her.

'Marco…' She murmured his name, hardly aware of what she wanted to say…all she could think about was the way he made her feel.

He leaned closer and suddenly his lips touched hers. The feeling was heavenly; she felt floodgates open inside her as she melted against the caress and kissed him back.

She couldn't remember the last man she had enjoyed kissing as much as this. It was certainly a long time since any other man had stirred up this rush of excitement, this dizzy feeling as adrenalin rushed through her veins. She reached up and put her hands on his shoulders.

By contrast, Marco's hands did not leave his sides. Even though she ached for him to touch her, he didn't, instead his kisses intensified, his mouth plundering hers with an expertise in seduction that was mind-blowing.

When he finally pulled away from her she was left throbbing with pure frustration.

'I meant it when I said there were no strings attached to dinner this evening. So unless you want to take this further I suggest we stop.'

Although he sounded firmly in control, one look into the

blaze of his dark eyes made her realise that he was holding on to his restraint by a thread.

She tried to think sensibly but it was difficult. 'Yes…of course. We have to work together and it would be madness to take things too far…'

'But an enjoyable kind of madness all the same,' he said teasingly. He stroked one hand softly down over the side of her face. The caress sent butterflies darting wildly inside her.

He lowered his head and kissed her again. 'I can't tell you how much I want you.' He murmured the words huskily against her mouth.

'I want you too.'

She heard herself say the words and yet felt no rush of panic, which was strange, considering how much deliberation she had been giving to this matter. In fact, all she felt as she looked into his eyes was an overwhelming sense that this was just *right*.

Marco smiled. 'Well, in that case…wouldn't it be madness *not* to take things further?' He kissed her again, this time with such a forceful, hungry passion that she was breathless as he pulled back.

'I think you're right,' she agreed tremulously. Then she looked up at him, a spark of mischief in the intense green of her eyes. 'But maybe you'd better kiss me again just so I can double-check…'

He laughed. 'You are a minx, Ms Charlotte Hopkirk, and you are driving me wild with desire…'

'That's good,' she smiled and pressed her lips to his, 'because you are having a similar effect on me…'

The next moment he had swung her up into his arms and was carrying her in a fireman's lift out of the room.

'Marco, put me down!' She was laughing breathlessly as he carried her up the stairs and into the bedroom opposite to hers.

'With pleasure.' He placed her down on the bed with a

playful thud. But as she looked up at him suddenly the laughter was gone and the atmosphere was very serious.

For a moment his gaze raked over her, taking in the soft fullness of her parted lips, the creamy flush on her high cheekbones, the sparkle in her eyes and the way her hair was spread out around her on the bed in wild, golden profusion.

Then his gaze moved lower towards the buttons on her dress.

'I've wanted you in my bed for some time, Charlie…' His voice held a husky rasp that she hadn't heard before; it sent tingles of awareness rushing through her.

Her heart thundered unsteadily. If they stepped over this line where would their relationship go from here?

Marco regarded her steadily. 'Are you having second thoughts?'

'No. I'm not having second thoughts. I'm just…' She struggled to express her feelings. She was scared, yet she couldn't stop things now.

'It's a while since you've done this, isn't it?' he said gently. 'Let me guess…it was with your husband just before he left?'

He saw the creaminess of her skin heat up and felt a dart of a fiercely protective emotion mingle with the animal desire that was eating him inside.

'Hey, it will be OK.' He bent over her and kissed her softly.

His velvet Italian tone seeped into her consciousness making her forget the momentary pangs of apprehension. Yes, it would be all right, she told herself as desire once more took her over. She wound her arms around his neck, and kissed him back with a sweet tenderness that seared into him.

His hands were on her body now, caressing her through the silky material of her dress. He felt her breasts tighten and harden beneath his touch, felt her acquiescence in every trembling, passionate kiss.

Pulling back from her, he peeled off his jumper and cast it

to one side. Underneath he was wearing a short-sleeved white T-shirt and it showed off the hard-muscled perfection of his broad shoulders and arms.

Hell but he had a fabulous body. She watched as his hand moved to unfasten the buckle on his leather belt.

Leaning up on one elbow, she took off her own belt and then kicked off her shoes. Then she started to unbutton her dress.

Marco had stopped undressing and was watching her now. She glanced up and saw the intense desire in his dark eyes and her heart thumped as if she had been running in a race. Suddenly her attempts to undress were slowed by hands that weren't at all steady or coordinated.

Marco smiled and reached out a hand to pull her up from the bed. 'Here, let me help.'

She allowed him to unfasten the last of the buttons and then stood silently in front of him as he pulled the dress from her shoulders and let it drop to the floor. Then his eyes moved with slow and thorough contemplation over the curves of her breasts in her black lacy bra before moving lower over her body and down across her stomach to the matching black knickers.

For a moment she felt acutely self-conscious as she suddenly wondered if he was comparing her voluptuous curves with the petite, perfect women he usually took to bed.

'You have a wonderful figure, Charlie,' he murmured. As he spoke he reached out a hand and trailed it lightly over the outline of her bra and she shivered with need.

She longed for him to really touch her, to caress her and kiss her, but instead he reached behind her and unfastened her bra, taking it from her with a slow deliberation that was tortuously provocative.

Apart from her lacy knickers she was naked now, whilst he was still almost fully dressed.

'Exquisitely sexy…' he murmured, his fingers trailing over

the side of her neck before moving lower to softly glide over the full, up-tilted firmness of her breasts.

Charlie closed her eyes on a wave of ecstasy as his lips started to follow the teasing, provocative trail down over the side of her neck and then lower until his lips found the hard, rosy peak of her nipple.

She drew in her breath on a gasp of pleasure and her hands moved upwards to rest against his shoulders. She could feel the warmth of his skin through the T-shirt and the tautness of his muscles.

He drew back from her for a moment and said something in Italian. But before she had a chance to ask what he had said he was pulling her underwear down, his hand lingering over the curves of her hips. Then, reaching behind her, he threw back the covers on the bed and gently pulled her down against the crisp white linen.

Lying sideways across the width of the bed, she watched as he pulled his T-shirt over his head. His skin was a deep golden bronze and smooth. Her eyes moved hungrily over the powerful torso and then lower towards his narrow hips. He was unzipping his jeans now.

Her heart was thundering fast and uneven against her chest. She wanted him so much…

'Hurry.' She breathed the word almost feverishly and he smiled.

'Patience, Charlotte,' he whispered teasingly.

'I don't want to be patient,' she complained huskily and he laughed. Leaving his jeans on, he straddled her. She could feel the coarse denim material against the soft flesh of her hips as he raised himself up, looking for something in his back pocket.

'Marco, really…' She writhed just a little beneath him, her senses on fire with longing. It felt as if there were a live volcano inside her and if he didn't get to it soon it was going to surely erupt without him. *'Hurry!'*

He brought out a foil packet and she realised that she had been so turned on that she had almost forgotten about contraception. He however, was very much in control. He was also *extremely* aroused, she noted as she watched him quickly remove his jeans and boxer shorts before deftly putting on the condom.

A moment later he leaned closer and found her lips. Then he kissed her in a way she had never been kissed before. It was hungry and passionate and so deeply arousing that it made her tingle deep inside her very core.

Murmuring words in Italian, he then kissed her face, trailing his heated, passionate lips down over her neck, whilst his hands possessively caressed her breasts.

Just when she thought that she couldn't wait another moment longer he entered her. The feeling was exquisite and the volcano of need inside her rose closer to the surface. She tried desperately to have some control over it so she could make the sensation go on and on for ever.

He stroked his hands over the soft roundness of her breasts, playing with her nipples and teasing their hardness with exquisite little butterfly kisses before taking them in his mouth. That was when she couldn't stand it any longer and she exploded in a million shattering, fantastic pieces.

She moaned a little and found herself gasping, then his lips moved to capture hers as if drinking in her shudders of ecstasy.

He held her close for a while, his hands tenderly soothing now as they moved over the silky softness of her skin.

She could smell the scent of his aftershave mixed with the clean smell of the linen. Nestling closer into the crook of his arm, she smiled sleepily.

'That was wonderful.' He growled the words against her ear and watched how her smile curved even more. 'You were worth waiting for.'

She cuddled closer and allowed her fingers to run over the powerful contours of his shoulder and his arm. It was blissful being held close like this. 'You certainly know how to please a woman,' she murmured sleepily.

He laughed. 'Well…what was it you said? If something is worth doing, it is worth doing well.'

She smiled and pressed her lips against his chest in a teasing kiss.

They lay entwined in each other's arms for a few moments more and then suddenly Marco pulled away from her.

'Where are you going?'

'I've just remembered that I forgot to put out the rest of the candles in the dining room. They have probably burnt out but I'd better go check.'

He stood up and pulled on his jeans.

'Hopefully the house isn't burning down.' He grinned over at her. 'I've already put out one fire today.'

She tossed one of the pillows from the bed over at him and he laughed as he disappeared.

Charlie repositioned herself in the bed and pulled the sheet over her. She had forgotten how lovely sex was…in fact, now she came to think about it, it really had never been as good as this with Greg.

Feeling sleepy and intoxicated with the afterglow of their lovemaking, she glanced around the room and saw the soft lamplight reflected over the bronze satin covers of the bed. Like her room across the corridor, there was a wood-burning stove in the corner and she could see the glow of flames flickering in the shadows. It felt cosy in here and blissfully quiet.

She closed her eyes and rested for a moment.

When Marco returned Charlie was fast asleep. He took off his clothes and slipped back into the bed beside her and for a while he watched as she slept.

There was an air of fragility about her, he thought. It was there in the softness of her smile and the way her hair was tousled in golden curls on the pillow around her head. Her eyelashes were dark and glossy against the smooth perfection of her skin. He reached out and trailed a finger over the silky smoothness of her shoulder. She stirred slightly and her lips curved into even more of a smile.

He was overwhelmed with a longing to take her again; it swept over him with a fierce intensity, taking him totally by surprise. Dipping his head, he trailed his lips along her shoulder and then upwards along her neck, breathing in the familiar scent of her perfume.

She smiled and murmured something sleepily.

'Hey, gorgeous…wake up!' His hand moved beneath the covers and slid over the satin of her skin. 'I want you…'

Her eyes flickered open and for a second their gazes held.

She was aware of a feeling inside her that was very strange. She felt as though she belonged here with him and that she wanted him to hold her against him and never let her go.

He kissed her gently, his lips sweetly provocative.

'The house hadn't burnt down, then?' she murmured sleepily.

'Not yet.' With a smile he pulled her closer, his hands coaxing and caressing her with slow deliberation, his kisses heated and yet tender.

The passion that flared between them was so intense and so pleasurable that she felt she couldn't get close enough to him. She just couldn't get enough of him.

A shiver stirred deep inside her. Emotions that were this intense were bound to have reverberations. The notion was fleeting though and was quickly taken away by the aching need that he stirred inside her with such ease.

Nothing mattered except this….

CHAPTER SEVEN

THE valley was shrouded in mist. It hung in the air like a mystical presence revealing only the faint gleam of the oyster-pink morning sky and the top of the lush green cypress trees on the hillside.

Somewhere a bell was chiming.

Charlie wrapped her silk dressing gown further around her body and on impulse opened the kitchen door and stepped onto the terrace. The morning air was cool and so fresh that she leaned against the stone parapet and took deep, revitalising breaths.

Behind her she could hear the bubble of water in the kettle on the stove. It was the only sound in the stillness of the morning.

As the sun rose from behind the mountain the oyster-pink of the sky turned flamingo and tinted the white mist with its brilliance. A hint of warmth stole across the day like the breath of summer.

Upstairs Marco was still sleeping in the warmth of the double bed. It had been an incredible night. Charlie had never known such passion. And lying wrapped in his arms afterwards had made her feel safe and contented and cherished... The thought made her frown. Of course, it was passion without love, she reminded herself firmly. So those feelings weren't correct.

It had just been sex—but the knowledge tore through her, causing an alarming feeling of pain.

Impatiently she raked a hand through the thickness of her blonde hair. This was what people in the real world did—they went to bed with someone they wanted and didn't analyse it afterwards…they just enjoyed the moment. So why couldn't she? Why were all these fragile emotions ricocheting through her?

Why had she woken up this morning and been filled with an aching void of need?

All she knew now was that she should never have gone to bed with him! It had been a mistake—a wonderful and very enjoyable mistake, but a mistake nonetheless. She should never have lowered her guard and allowed her weakness for him to get the better of her. All it had done was to leave her wanting more from him on a deeper emotional level and that was one thing she knew Marco would never be able to give.

A sound from behind made her turn around. Marco was in the doorway, watching her. Their eyes met and held and for a few breathless moments the memory of what had happened lay between them with a sensual heat.

His dark hair was still tousled from sleep and he was wearing a pair of black pyjama bottoms and nothing else. How was it that he looked even sexier when he was disheveled? she wondered. She longed to go over and kiss him, and smooth his hair back from his face with tender fingers. But actions like that were not for the cool light of morning. In fact, she couldn't ever allow herself to act like that around him again, she told herself fiercely.

How was she going to work with him now? she wondered in anguish. How would she ever get back to a place of safety where she could pretend indifference?

'Buon giorno, Charlie.'

The velvety Italian tones made her want to melt. Hell, but this was no good! She was going to have to pull herself together.

'How are you feeling this morning?' he enquired with a lift of one eyebrow.

'Fine…I slept really well.' She tried very hard to match his casual, laid-back manner.

'You got up very early.'

'I couldn't wait to have a look outside at the view,' she lied. In truth she had made herself leave the warmth of his arms because she had liked being there too much, and she couldn't bear the fact that he might wake and see that in her eyes.

'Would you like a coffee?' she asked now trying to be cool and collected.

'*Si.*' Marco watched as she made her way carefully around him and went back into the kitchen.

His eyes flicked over her, taking in her bare feet before moving upwards over the curvy silhouette of her figure. Then they lingered on her face. He noticed not for the first time that she didn't need make-up. Her skin was fresh and clear and had a kind of luminous quality. Her lips were a soft peach and her hair tumbled in a sexy cascade over her shoulders. He remembered how she had felt beneath his touch, the silk of her skin, the heat of her passion. He had enjoyed every moment of last night and she had left him wanting more.

Charlie was acutely conscious of the fact that his dark eyes were moving over her with that boldly assessing gaze of his. She wished she had brushed her hair before coming downstairs…because she was sure the dishevelled look didn't do her any favours, unlike him.

She raised her chin a little as she looked over at him. 'You are making me a bit nervous,' she admitted suddenly.

'Am I?' He looked at her with amusement. 'Why is that?'

'Because you are looking at me with such concentration! And it's too early in the morning for that. I need at least an hour getting ready before I can pass such scrutiny!'

Marco laughed. 'You are very amusing, Charlie!'

She shot him an impatient look. She didn't want to be amusing! She wanted to be gorgeous and beautiful and all the things that drove him wild…the way he drove her wild. The thought made her angry with herself. Why should she care what he thought? She needed to get real. Last night was about sex and nothing more.

'What's with that look?' he asked softly.

'What look?' She put his coffee down on the counter beside him.

'That *I'm not taking any of your nonsense* look.'

Despite herself, Charlie laughed, she couldn't help herself. 'And you say I'm amusing!'

'Do you regret last night?'

The question caught her off guard. She couldn't look at him now. 'No, it was…fun.' She tried very hard to sound unruffled. 'I just think we need to concentrate on more important things now.' It took every last ounce of strength to make herself look up at him. 'We have work to do this morning.'

She noted an edge of approval now in the dark, steady gaze that held hers and she realised that she had unwittingly reinforced the idea that she was in tune with his theories…that practicality had to come above emotion. She was obviously a better actress than she had imagined, she thought sardonically.

'You're right, of course.' He reached out and trailed a finger softly over the side of her face, tracing its contours as if committing them to memory. And suddenly she just wanted to forget any pretence and go back into his arms again, and to hell with practicality.

'But after a night like last night we really should say good morning properly.'

The provocative note in his voice and the way he was looking at her sent darts of awareness and need instantly racing through her. She tried desperately to ignore them but they didn't want to leave. 'You mean…*buon giorno?*' She tried to make light of his words and copied his Italian with a smile.

'That's very good,' he murmured, tracing one finger over the softness of her lips. 'I could make an Italian out of you yet. But I was thinking more along the lines of actions speaking louder than words...'

Then he bent his head and kissed her. It was the most fabulous sensation—possessive and sensual and spine-tingling all at the same time. For a moment she found herself kissing him back, then reality started to seep in and she realised that this was a mistake. This shouldn't happen again. She couldn't allow herself to get pulled further into a situation she couldn't cope with.

Because the fact was that she was a million miles away from ever being in tune with Marco's theories and his cool, carefree attitude towards love and sex would just annihilate an old-fashioned hearts-and-flowers girl like her.

Hastily she pulled away from him. 'We need to draw a line under this now, Marco, and get back to how things should be.'

'Of course.' He agreed with her immediately, and she noticed that, unlike her, he was completely relaxed. He glanced at his watch. 'I'll go shower and get dressed and we'll meet downstairs in my office in, say, half an hour. How does that sound?'

'Fine.' She swallowed hard. In reality she wanted to go upstairs and lock herself away for the rest of the weekend. She really didn't know how she was going to maintain a professional distance after this. Hurriedly she picked up her coffee and turned away.

Marco watched her go with a look of deep contemplation in his eyes. He was well aware that she wanted to pull up her barriers now and close him out but, while he was content to allow her to do that for the business side of their relationship, he had no intention of allowing her to retreat from him completely. He had worked too hard to reach her for that. He had other plans for Charlie.

* * *

'Will you take a copy of these notes?' Marco put a stack of papers down in front of her. 'Oh, and try and get Professor Hunt on the phone. I could do with talking to him about our meeting on Sunday.'

'I'll get on to it straight away.' Charlie reached for the desk diary. This was really weird, she thought as she leafed through the pages to find the professor's number. Somehow their professional barriers were in place…somehow they had been working alongside each other all morning as if nothing had happened last night.

Charlie couldn't quite figure out how they were managing it. Maybe it was the fact that they were in a room that was very reminiscent of Marco's office in London. Or maybe it was just the way Marco could totally tune in to his work with a single-minded absorption, something that had always fascinated her about him.

She put his call through, then got up to switch on the scanner. Marco's velvet tones resonated through the book-lined room as he talked to his colleague. She glanced over at him, momentarily distracted from what she was doing. Even when he was talking about business he sounded sexy.

As if sensing her gaze he glanced up and their eyes collided. The impact made her stomach contract with a sudden need that hit her out of nowhere. Hurriedly she looked away and tried to concentrate on what she was doing as he finished his conversation.

'I think we are just about finished here,' Marco said a few moments later as he replaced the receiver. 'The rest of it can wait until we get back to London.'

Charlie collected the copies that were churning out from the machine. He was right—they had managed to sail through everything in a relatively short space of time. The trouble was, she didn't want to step out from behind the screen of work. 'You've got to sign the letters on your desk,' she reminded him.

'I will do it later.' He stood up and glanced at his watch. 'Time to go out.'

She frowned. 'Actually, Marco—'

'It's a beautiful day and I did promise you that there would be time for sightseeing.' He cut across her as if she hadn't spoken. 'And you can't come all the way to Tuscany and not see Florence. It would be a sin.'

The matter-of-fact tone dented her reservations. She really would like to see Florence. And at least if they were in a city they would be surrounded by other people, so it was hardly high-risk for seduction!

'OK…but do you mind if I phone home first? I'd like to check everything is all right with Jack.'

'Sure.' He smiled. 'Use the landline.'

They left the villa half an hour later. The sun was shimmering down from a clear blue sky and a heat haze danced over the winding roads. Charlie was glad that she had taken the time to change out of her trouser suit into a dress. She felt summery in the feminine blue and white creation.

Relaxing back in the comfortable leather seat, she watched as the countryside passed by and told herself that she was only going to think about the scenery…nothing else.

In the distance a mountain village dazzled the senses with shimmering gold turrets amidst a profusion of terracotta roofs. Vineyards criss-crossed the land in geometric patterns, the grapes incandescent and heavy, ripened by long months of sunshine.

They stopped for coffee before heading on towards Florence, the Tuscany capital. And instead of the mood between them being tense or uncertain there was a surprising light-hearted feeling of exhilaration. They found themselves laughing over the most trivial of things, and suddenly just enjoying the moment was all that seemed to matter.

Charlie didn't think she would ever forget that day, strolling around in the heat of the sun, marvelling at the architecture, the medieval churches, the art and history of the city blending so easily together. They ate lunch outside at a pavement café and then lingered over a glass of Chianti as they watched the people go by.

After lunch Charlie shopped for some presents to bring home. Marco watched as she deliberated carefully over what to buy Jack.

'Which do you think I should get?' She held up a shiny red remote-control car and a boxed game.

'I think the car,' he said firmly. 'Jack loves cars.'

'Yes…but the game is educational, it will teach him something about Italy. Plus it looks fun.'

'Then you should get both.' Marco smiled.

'Just what I was thinking.' She put the toys in the shopping basket, a gleam of enjoyment in her eyes. 'He'll be really thrilled.'

There was something very…endearing about Charlie, Marco thought as he followed her further around the shop. He noticed she'd caught the sun today and had a sprinkling of freckles over her nose now. She really was very attractive. Not magazine-model beautiful but seductively alluring in a much warmer and interesting way.

He liked the lively glint in her eyes that spoke of intelligence and good humour…and the way her lips curved upwards; so soft and sensual. He even liked the way she was taking so much trouble over choosing the perfect presents for Jack.

Things were really working out quite well. She was great in bed, plus she was very businesslike—a wonderful combination.

He tried to pay for her purchases at the till but she wouldn't hear of it.

'I didn't realise you could be quite so bossy,' he said as they stepped back outside onto the pavement.

'I didn't mean to be. It was kind of you to offer to pay but I don't know why you did—'

'Because I *wanted* to.' He reached to carry her bags for her and grinned teasingly. 'Truth is, I quite fancied the car myself. I'd have given my right arm for that when I was a boy.'

She laughed. 'Well, you can come around and play any time.' She knew she shouldn't be flirting with him like this…but the spark of mischief in her felt good.

'Now, there's a promise and a half!' He looked at her with a raised eyebrow and she felt a thrill of emotion deep inside.

As they strolled back towards the car he casually reached to take her hand in his.

It was a nonchalant, relaxed gesture but to Charlie the possessive touch was deliciously intoxicating and it made her heart warm with pleasure. It was a long time since she had felt like this around someone.

As they paused by the kerb a motorbike suddenly pulled up in front of them and two men jumped off with cameras in their hands.

'Marco…' They called to him, and said something in Italian.

Charlie looked over in astonishment as they started to take rapid pictures of them crossing the road. 'What on earth are they playing at?'

'It's the paparazzi.' Marco squeezed her hand. 'Don't worry about it,' he said easily. 'We are nearly back at the car now. I suggest we head out of the city and get away from them.'

She nodded wordlessly.

'Sorry, I should have warned you about the photographers,' Marco said casually as they left the heat and noise of Florence behind and drove out in the direction of Sienna. 'That kind of thing is happening quite a lot recently.'

'Yes…I suppose it is.' Charlie frowned. Marco was so down-to-earth that she had forgotten that she was with a celebrity.

He looked over at her. 'You're not bothered by it, are you?'

'No. I just hope they snapped my good side,' she added flippantly.

Marco laughed. 'Well, as you don't have a bad side, I think you're safe.'

The country roads they took were through the majesty of winding hills with olive groves, old cottages and castles. Cypress trees stood guard against the fierce blue skyline.

They stopped the car to allow a shepherd to herd his goats out across the road and Marco glanced in the rear-view mirror. 'You can relax now, we seem to have lost them.'

'I was relaxed,' she murmured. 'It would take more than a few photographers to ruin such a lovely day.'

'You're right.' Marco glanced over at her, a gleam of approbation in his dark eyes. 'You know, asking you to come to Italy with me was a great idea,' he said softly.

She looked over at him and tried not to be carried away by the depth of sincerity in his gaze. 'Well, we managed to get through all that work this morning quite quickly.'

'I was thinking about more than just the work we got through.'

For a moment their eyes held. And suddenly the atmosphere seemed to change from teasing warmth to something else…something much more serious.

She felt her heart thudding so hard against her chest it felt as if it were going to explode. This was the point when she should move back, she told herself. But when he leaned across towards her she didn't do any such thing, instead she allowed him to take her into his arms and kiss her with a passion that was overwhelming.

This was how she wanted life to be, Charlie thought hazily. Nights of love in Marco's arms and snatched moments like this. Maybe she should stop fighting it and just enjoy an affair with him.

The idea sizzled through her, causing immediate consternation. What on earth was she thinking about? An affair was all very well…but it wouldn't last for more than a few weeks. She had seen for herself how quickly Marco lost interest in women. And even if the affair lasted months instead of weeks she wouldn't be able to cope with Marco's cool take on emotions. It would tear her apart. Plus it would put a strain on her job. Allowing herself to believe otherwise was just inviting heartache.

She pulled away from him abruptly. 'Listen, Marco…last night was great but—'

'But I had better curtail my animal passions…hmm?' He drawled the words softly.

'I think it's for the best.' Her voice was distracted. 'I don't think we should let it happen again.'

He reached out and touched her face. 'I'm not so sure about that.'

The words sent little quivering darts of pleasure racing right through her body.

And as she looked into his eyes she realised exactly why she couldn't have an affair with him. The truth was, it would never be enough because she was falling in love with him.

The knowledge hit her out of nowhere and it sent shock waves pulsating through her entire system.

Maybe Marco had been right all along, she thought in panic…maybe when sex came into play you couldn't trust emotions…couldn't trust feelings to be correct, because surely she couldn't be this foolish?

She knew Marco's feelings on this subject! He wasn't looking for emotional involvement…. In fact that was the last thing he wanted.

And she didn't want it either. She knew how painful love could be when it all went wrong…and it could never work with Marco. They might be sexually suited but in emotional terms they were poles apart.

She was supposed to be Ms Practicality, she reminded herself scornfully. To Marco last night was just a fling—a bit of fun—and he believed she had the same ethos. If he even guessed what was running through her mind now he would be horrified.

'Charlie, are you OK?'

He was looking at her with questioning eyes.

'Yes, of course I'm OK,' she made herself reply cheerfully.

A car horn blared behind them and Marco glanced abruptly away. He saw that the road was now clear and he was now holding up a line of cars behind him.

He quickly put the engine into gear and the powerful car moved forward. 'Anyway we'll talk more over dinner. There is a *trattoria* further along this road. We'll stop there.'

Charlie made no reply; she was too busy listening to her heart telling her she was completely out of her depth here.

CHAPTER EIGHT

As THEY pulled up outside a rustic *trattoria* the sun was starting to dip down behind the mountains, sending long shadows over the rolling plains. And with the setting sun there was a sudden coolness in the air.

Charlie shivered a little as she stepped out of the car but she wasn't sure if it was from the evening air…or her thoughts. She really needed to pull herself together, she thought crossly.

It was a relief to be greeted by a lively, buzzing atmosphere inside the restaurant. At least if she was a little quieter than usual Marco might not notice.

A waiter hurried over to greet them, talking rapidly in Italian.

Charlie listened as Marco answered in a slower, more measured tone. She loved the sound of his voice when he spoke in English but when he spoke in his own language it was an incredible turn-on.

She remembered how he had spoken in Italian to her as they made love last night…whispering the hot words in her ear as he took her higher and higher into spasms of pleasure.

Desperately she tried to shut those memories away.

The waiter led them to a secluded alcove with views out of the window towards the setting sun.

'I take it you are a regular here when you're home?' Charlie tried to keep the light tone in her voice as she sat down opposite to him.

'Yes. It's convenient for the villa and the food is excellent.'

'I love Italian food.' She flicked open the menu and pretended to study it with every shred of her concentration. But in truth she couldn't concentrate or even see very well. The lighting was low and she really needed to put her glasses on…something she was loath to do around him.

'Yes, Italian food does rate high on the list of life's pleasures,' Marco agreed easily. 'Along with good company and passionate interludes; all of which have made this trip perfect.'

She glanced over and as their eyes held Charlie tried very hard to rationalise all the feelings that suddenly flowed through her with vivid intensity.

It would be very easy to read all the wrong signals from that intense gaze. Just as it would be easy to imagine that what had transpired between them in the bedroom was serious.

But it wasn't.

He had just referred to last night as *a passionate interlude.* She needed to take heed of what was real and what was imagined. He'd probably brought numerous women for such interludes to his house, and here to this restaurant, she reminded herself. The thought twisted unpleasantly inside her. 'Yes, it's been fun while it's lasted,' she said coolly.

Hurriedly she looked away from him and tried to focus on the noisy bustle and repartee of the waiters, and the roaring open wood-fired ovens where the chef was baking bread.

Marco wondered why Charlie was suddenly so tense and withdrawn. For a while this afternoon he had really thought he had won her around again, as she had been so relaxed and open.

He watched as she opened her handbag and put her reading-glasses on. She looked very cute in them and he liked the way her nose wrinkled a little as she concentrated. He was suddenly filled with an almost irresistible urge to reach out and touch her, to smooth the little frown lines away. He forced himself to pull back, sensing that if he didn't handle this right she could withdraw completely.

She glanced over and caught him watching her.

'You look good in your glasses,' he said smoothly.

'I've been told that they make me look too serious.' She glanced back towards the menu. She didn't want him to start lying to her. One of the things she liked about Marco was his honesty.

'Really? Who told you that?'

She shrugged. It was her ex-husband but she didn't want to tell him that. 'I can't remember. Does it matter?'

'No, except I wouldn't take any fashion tips from whoever it was. Because you look lovely…incredibly sexy, in fact.'

His voice held a husky honesty that tore at her defences.

'You are just a charmer, Marco,' she managed to say primly and switched the subject. 'Now, although I can now see the menu, I can't understand it…'

He smiled and leaned a little closer. She could smell the scent of his cologne, intoxicating and warmly provocative. It made her remember what is was like to be held in his arms.

Somehow she managed to make herself concentrate on the blithe conversation and laugh with Marco as he helped her to translate some of the dishes.

They placed their orders and Marco reached to pour her a glass of wine. Outside darkness stole over the countryside and the flicker of candlelight lit the room.

'So are you all prepared for your TV interview tomorrow?' Charlie asked, taking the lead in the conversation. She was determined not to let things slip towards anything personal.

'Just about…' He paused for a second and then to Charlie's relief followed her lead. And suddenly they were back on safe ground again, talking about work.

'Of course, when you join me in America for the interviews there it will be pretty hectic. Not much time for sightseeing, I'm afraid.'

The line was thrown casually into the conversation but it caused an immense wave of consternation inside her. 'You want me to go to America with you?'

'Well, I'll need you to join me for a few days in New York. Nothing more than that.'

'Oh!' Her heart was thumping wildly again and the feeling that she was out of her depth resurfaced with violent intensity.

'I did tell you that I would need you to accompany me on a few business trips.' He looked over at her with a frown.

'Yes…but I assumed you might need me at the conference in Edinburgh for a day…that kind of thing.'

'No, I'll be relying on you to run the office while I'm in Edinburgh. I'm expecting some important files around that time and you'll need to categorise them.' He looked at her very seriously now. 'But after that I want you to fly to New York and join me for three, maybe four days. I take it that won't be a problem?'

The light in his eyes and the no-nonsense tone suddenly reminded her in no uncertain terms that this was her boss. They might have enjoyed a fling last night but he certainly didn't expect it to get in the way of work. He wouldn't be impressed about her crossing the line and letting him down.

'Of course not,' she said quickly. This was business, she reminded herself as she fought down the feelings of apprehension. She had already agreed to a few trips and there was no way she could lose this job.

'Good.' He smiled at her and the fleeting steel-like mood was gone, replaced with a warm gleam of approval. 'Because our working arrangements are going very well, I think.'

'Yes…' She frowned. If only she could get past these personal feelings they would be perfect.

They talked for a while longer about work. She relaxed back. Everything would be fine, she told herself staunchly.

Marco was right about the food—the antipasto was mouth-wateringly good.

'Why is it that pasta doesn't taste as good as this at home?' she asked as the waiter cleared away their empty plates to put their main course down.

'Probably because it's made fresh here.' Marco shrugged. 'But, of course, you can find good pasta in England…if you know where to go.'

'And where is that?' She glanced over at him with interest.

'Around to my place for dinner, naturally,' he said with a smile.

She wished she didn't feel that instant flare of warmth at that suggestion. 'That's what I like about you—you're so modest,' she murmured, but she couldn't help but smile over at him.

'So shall we call that a provisional date some time?' Marco reached and took a sip of his drink.

'Maybe…' She tried to match his casual tone. He was just teasing, she told herself. 'If we can find a space in the diary.'

He smiled. 'And that's what I like about you…'

'What's that?' She glanced over at him warily.

'The fact that you always have your feet on the ground and are so totally practical, of course.'

Although it was just a light-hearted remark, there was a serious edge to it. Charlie knew that…

'Of course.' She avoided his gaze and pretended to concentrate on her meal.

And his belief that she was so practical in all areas of her life was why a relationship between them wouldn't work out.

'The fact that you are still very sexy without the glasses is also quite a draw,' he added with a spark of devilment.

She looked over at him and wished she were the person he imagined…an ultra-modern career girl who didn't allow herself to be ruled by emotions. She wished she really could just view sex as a recreational enjoyment instead of something serious. She wished she could go back to bed with him tonight and not worry about where it was leading.

'Have you ever been in love, Marco?' She asked the question impulsively.

He regarded her quizzically for a moment. 'Why do you ask?'

'I don't know… I guess I'm just curious.' She shrugged and felt suddenly self-conscious. She probably shouldn't have asked him that!

'I lived with someone once,' he answered slowly. 'We met at university and shared an apartment for two years.'

Charlie looked at him in surprise. 'Really?'

'Yes. We considered marriage and then we realised that we weren't suited, that we both wanted different things out of life.'

'You didn't want to make the commitment to her?' Charlie guessed.

'It was a mutual decision.'

Somehow Charlie didn't believe that.

'Some people just aren't cut out for marriage,' he said with a shrug. 'And it's all too easy to get swept along by passion and emotion and forget that. Fortunately we didn't and because of that we have managed to remain good friends.'

'That takes some doing!'

'Not really.' Marco frowned. 'We are very much on an academic wavelength. So usually when we meet up it is to discuss our work.'

Charlie was surprised to find a flicker of jealousy curl inside her and she hastily pushed the feeling away. She wasn't the jealous type and she wasn't going to start now. 'It's surprising the relationship didn't work out…when you had so much in common,' she said lightly.

'Well, it didn't.' He looked over at her steadily.

Charlie told herself to leave the subject alone. It was none of her business, but somehow she just couldn't. 'So why do you think that was?'

For a moment he didn't answer her.

'I guess you broke her heart,' she added flippantly.

Marco laughed at that, but the sound held none of his usual warmth. 'Well, then, you would be wrong. The relationship broke down when I was away on business. Maria went out with friends one evening and met up with an old flame. She had a one-night fling with him.'

Charlie was totally taken aback, not just by the fact that any woman would want to cheat on someone as gorgeous as Marco but also by a glimpse of some stark emotion in his eyes—an emotion she had never seen there before.

'So how did you find out about it?' she asked curiously.

Marco shrugged. 'She felt guilty and told me.'

'So it really was just a one-night fling?'

'Yes.' Marco held her gaze impassively. 'But if the relationship had been right she wouldn't have felt tempted to stray. Obviously there were flaws that needed to be addressed, and when we looked into it we realised that the flaws were too deep to continue with the relationship.'

'I see…' Charlie watched him across the table and saw the flicker of darkness in his expression. Betrayal was something he couldn't handle. The realisation flashed in her mind and suddenly she understood Marco's wariness where commitment was concerned. Obviously watching his parents tearing each other apart had made him cautious and then Maria had reinforced that.

This was why he was so determined not to get emotionally involved.

Unexpectedly the insight lit a small ray of hope inside her. *Maybe if Marco found someone he could trust he would allow himself to fall in love and he would start to change his views about emotional commitment. Maybe he would start to believe in its power for the good.* The thought brushed through Charlie's mind. *Maybe he just hadn't found the right person.*

She liked the idea…but then again, she would, she thought drily. She was a romantic.

'Now…do you think we could leave the past alone?' He reached across and took hold of her hand. 'Because I've got other more pressing interests right now, and I'm not talking about work either.'

The touch of his hand on hers sent little darts of desire racing through her from nowhere. But for once she didn't feel the need to pull away from him. In fact she actually felt a tentative need to respond to him. Like her, Marco had been hurt, and maybe if she could prove to him that he could rely on her and trust her then maybe one day he might open up to her the way she had to him.

She knew it was a risky strategy. Marco didn't allow himself to get involved with anyone for long. But by virtue of working with him, she was closer to him than anyone had been in a while. Maybe it would give her a slight edge.

'Do you know what I would like right at this moment?' he murmured huskily.

'What's that?'

'I'd like to take you home…undress you very, very slowly and then kiss you all over…' As he was speaking his thumb traced little circles over the inside curve of her arm. It was a deliciously erotic feeling.

The last of her reservations fell away.

'I think I'd like that too,' she admitted softly.

When Charlie woke the next morning she was curled up in the protective warmth of Marco's arms. The sun was slanting in through the open curtains and the only sound was the sweet trill of birdsong in the morning air.

She smiled and buried herself deeper into Marco's arms. She loved being here with him like this. Languid memories of their lovemaking flicked through her mind. They had barely made it home from the restaurant before they had started to tear each other's clothes off. If she looked up from the pillow she knew she would see a trail of clothing leading from the door.

Their lovemaking had been intensely passionate and unlike anything Charlie had ever experienced in her marriage. Marco could arouse her with such ease.

The first night she had tried to tell herself that the intensity of pleasure she had experienced was because she hadn't made love for so long. But now she knew that this was just the way Marco was able to make her feel. It was incredible and addictive and the more she thought about it…the more she wanted him all over again.

She tilted her head and studied him as he slept, her eyes moving over the aristocratically handsome face and taking in every detail.

Even in sleep he looked powerful…like a sleeping tiger. But she knew the truth, she thought with a zing of pleasure. Marco wasn't as cool and composed as he liked to pretend. He had a vulnerable edge. Like her, he had just built up his own set of defences to hide the fact. How to find a way around those defences was the question that was occupying her this morning.

He opened his eyes suddenly and caught her watching him. She noticed the golden flecks in their dark depths.

'*Buon giorno.*' She whispered the words softly, her voice shy.

He smiled sleepily and, brushing a hand through her long hair he reached and kissed her tenderly on the lips.

Her naked body was crushed against his and she could feel his arousal. He rolled her over, pressing her down against the softness of the mattress as he kissed the side of her face, her neck, before his lips moved lower…

Her hands raked through the darkness of his hair. And she closed her eyes on a wave of pleasure as once more he made love to her with a thorough passion that made her dizzy and made her gasp his name…

As always Marco was totally in control, steadying her, soothing her, kissing her senseless until she was almost begging for release. He smiled as he took her to climax… raking hungry, possessive hands over her body, claiming her and making her totally his.

Then as she collapsed weakly against him, clinging to him, her body damp, her senses swimming, he suddenly pulled away and looked at the clock on the bedside table.

'Is that the correct time?'

Charlie could hardly think coherently, never mind look at the time. She glanced blearily at her watch. 'I think it's eight-thirty.'

'Damn! I'd better get moving.' He threw the covers back and got out of bed. 'I've got to be at the TV station for my interview in less than an hour!'

She snuggled back down against the pillows, watching as he threw a robe around his shoulders.

'Hey, don't get too comfortable!' He threw her a smile. 'I want you to come with me.'

Charlie groaned. 'I feel like staying in bed. You've worn me out.'

He laughed. 'Sorry, but we've got a plane to catch…and we'll have to leave straight from the TV station.'

Back to reality… The unwelcome thought crept in. What was going to happen when they got home? Would she be able to hold on to this tentatively wonderful feeling that was spiralling between them?

He sat down on the side of the bed suddenly and looked at her. 'By the way,' he drawled lazily, 'just in case I forget to tell you, I've enjoyed every minute of this weekend with you.' He punctuated the sentence with a lingering softly sensual kiss.

'I've enjoyed it too.' She felt her heart thumping loudly against her chest. There were no sentimental words of love and she didn't for one moment expect that. But telling her how much he enjoyed every minute was the next best thing…wasn't it? At least he was honest and she respected him for that.

She wound her arms around his neck and kissed him back. Maybe she could handle this situation. She'd have to do a great job of acting when she got home…pretend that she wasn't head-over-heels in love and that she was in tune with his thinking on romance. It would be worth it though, she thought dreamily…if Marco opened up to her and allowed her into his life.

He pulled away from her. 'Right, come on…' He tugged the sheet. 'My public awaits…'

She laughed breathlessly. 'If they could see you now!'

'It might do wonders for my profile,' he teased as he went through towards the dressing room and the *en suite* bathroom. 'It would certainly please Sarah…which reminds me, I promised to phone her this morning.'

The very name of Sarah Heart encroaching in on the day was enough to send shadows over it.

She heard Marco turning on the shower in the next room and at the same time the phone beside the bed rang.

'I bet that's her!' Marco shouted. 'Answer it, will you, Charlie? Tell her I'm in the shower and I'll phone her back later.'

Pulling a face, she rolled over and lifted the receiver.

Marco was right; it was Sarah, and her breathy, cheerful voice was just as grating as ever. 'Hi, Marco; how's it going?' she gushed. 'Hope everything is on track for a really great interview this morning.'

'Actually, Sarah, it's Charlie,' she answered. 'Marco's in the shower, can he ring you back?'

There was a slight pause before Sarah continued in the same cheerful tone. 'Oh, hello, Charlie. How is your weekend going?'

'It's going fine, thank you.' Charlie frowned. It was unlike Sarah to try and make polite conversation.

'Having a nice *romantic* time?'

Was it her imagination or was there a definite sarcastic edge to Sarah's voice now?

'Well, we've been working…but we are *both* having a wonderful time,' she answered coolly.

'Well, you certainly look like a real couple…and as I said to Marco, that's what really counts. It's all about getting the right spin on a situation, and he's certainly doing that with lots of hand-holding and smouldering glances…great.'

A cold feeling was starting to churn inside Charlie now. 'What on earth are you talking about?'

'Sorry, Charlie, I'm rambling, aren't I? I'm looking at the photograph of you and Marco strolling hand in hand through the streets of Florence. It's in the morning papers. And I'm just so pleased. It's great publicity.'

'Well, I'm *so* glad you're pleased.' Charlie tried to keep her voice on an even keel but her brain was racing frantically and anger was starting to rise. Words like *spin* and *great publicity* were whirring around like instruments of torture. 'But I can assure you we were just enjoying ourselves.'

'Well, that's a relief, because when I set up the photo and suggested this I was a bit hesitant. I mean, you never really know how these things will work out, do you? And Marco was very reluctant to follow my ideas at first…well, you know what he's like, so stubborn…and didn't like the idea of getting tied into a romantic involvement even as a publicity stunt.'

Charlie felt her heart go into freefall. 'Yes, I know what he's like,' she said numbly. Had Marco known the photographers were going to snap them yesterday? Had he got her to Italy on false pretences? Seduced her and used her as some kind of publicity stunt to promote his book?

'Anyway, I just knew that you would be the perfect foil for him,' Sarah continued merrily. 'Especially when he mentioned that he felt comfortable around you and that you were on a similar wavelength, that's why we decided that a short

weekend in Italy would be a good starting point for you both—
you know, just to test the waters.'

We decided? The words ricocheted through Charlie. Marco
had discussed her with Sarah…had invited her here *on Sarah's
suggestion?*

'Has he asked you to go to America with him yet?' Sarah
asked suddenly. 'Seeing it's going so well, I'm sure he will.
And that would be brilliant, Charlie…it will really help having
you in the background just to overset these awkward questions
about his personal life.'

Charlie felt sick. Where the hell had her brain been these
last few days? All these years of playing things safe and now
it looked as if she had walked straight into a damn set-up…she
had allowed herself to be used. *She had fallen in love with a
man who thought nothing of her…a man who had discussed
her and probably laughed about her behind her back.*

'Charlie, are you still there?' Sarah asked with a smile in
her voice. 'You've gone awfully quiet.'

Fury was starting to take over from heartache. She had
always known that Sarah Heart was a complete bitch—she was
enjoying this! She was also probably totally eaten up with
jealousy, Charlie reminded herself. Maybe this wasn't even
true. Maybe Marco knew nothing about Sarah's plans for the
photographers to catch them!

'Yes…I'm here…to be honest with you I'm falling
asleep.' Charlie managed to fake a yawn, a yawn that felt
achingly as if it wanted to turn into tears. 'Marco and I have
been enjoying a weekend of wild passion…in fact things
have progressed out of all control between us. It's been absolutely fantastic.'

'That's great.'

Charlie felt a little better as she heard Sarah's voice drop a
decibel of cheer.

'Yes, it has been great…so *if* you've suggested this then

thank you so much from both of us. Anyway, better go now. *Marco needs me....* He'll phone you if he gets time.'

She slammed down the phone and just lay there, her heart thundering with fury and hurt.

What was the truth behind this situation? Was Sarah making things up?

Marco had told her up front about Sarah's publicity ideas for his book. What was it he had said that day in the car? *'Having a suitable partner around at the moment wouldn't go amiss.'* He'd even gone so far as to tell her that as his book tour started in five weeks, he probably wouldn't be able to find a suitable candidate in time.

And what had she had said? *'Oh, I'm sure you will be able to dig up someone acceptable very quickly.'*

Charlie cringed. God, it looked as though Sarah was telling the truth...and she had walked right into it with her lies about being on his wavelength!

She remembered her first instinct regarding involvement with Marco had been wariness. She had known it would suit his purposes to have someone like her around, but somewhere along the line she had let go of those concerns and she had honestly thought that he'd invited her here just in her capacity as PA. And that night when he'd made dinner for her and they had relaxed together she had imagined that there was a genuine connection between them.

But now little things that he had said to her over the last few weeks started to trickle with chilling emphasis through her mind.

When he had taken her out for lunch on that first day, he'd said, *'Where you and I are concerned, business and pleasure could fit together very nicely.'*

And yesterday when he'd mentioned her joining him in America he'd looked implacable, as if the trip was all-important. What was it he had said? *'Our working arrangements are going very well, I think.'*

And to think that deep down she had imagined he really was attracted to her! How stupid was she? The truth had been staring her in the face and she hadn't chosen to see it…why hadn't she chosen to ask herself why someone like Marco would suddenly want to spend time with her?

Instead she had naïvely been fooling herself into thinking a relationship with him might stand a chance!

As Marco returned to the room Charlie snatched up her dressing gown and wrapped it around her body with shaking fingers.

He was wearing a dark suit that sat perfectly on his broad-shouldered frame, making him look dangerously attractive and powerfully compelling. She felt her stomach flip over.

Marco could have his pick of the most glamorous and beautiful women but he had chosen her because he deemed her safe and *comfortable*. He thought she was Ms Practicality, who wouldn't get carried away by emotion or expect more from him than he wanted to give.

'Was that Sarah on the phone?' he asked as he strolled across to the wardrobe to flick through a rack of ties.

'Yes; I said you'd ring her back.'

'Thanks.' He selected a silver tie and started to put it on. 'Hurry up, Charlie.' He slanted a wry look over as she made no attempt to leave the room. 'You haven't got long to get ready!'

'I'm aware of that.' Her voice wasn't entirely steady. 'Marco, did you know those photographers were going to be around yesterday?' She had to hear the truth from him so she could know for sure if what Sarah had told her was correct.

He didn't appear to miss a beat, just continued to fasten his tie. 'Why are you asking me that now? I told you…they are always around these days.'

'Yes, but did you specifically arrange with Sarah for that photograph to be taken yesterday?'

Marco looked at her now. 'She did mention something about it…' His voice was casually indifferent. 'But I told you, didn't I, that she wants to spice up my profile romantically?'

Fury lashed through her at that casual admission. 'Yes, you did. I just didn't realise that I was the spice in question.' Her voice was laced with sarcasm.

To her annoyance Marco merely looked amused by the accusation. He met her clear green gaze and then shook his head. 'I thought you didn't mind about the photographs? When I asked, you said it didn't matter.'

'It didn't matter when it was an unforeseen incident…it matters a hell of a lot more when you deliberately set me up for it!' Her eyes were blazing into his now.

'I didn't set you up for it!' he said calmly.

'Oh, sorry…let's get this right. *Both* of you set me up for it. In fact…you only asked me to come to Italy with you in the first place to test the waters…ready for the big PR exercise in America.'

A sudden look of anger passed over Marco's dark features. 'Did Sarah say that?'

'Yes, she damn well did!' Charlie wished that her voice hadn't faltered at that moment. 'Not that I care or anything.' She lifted her chin defiantly. 'But you should have been more honest with me…'

'Charlie, I was honest with you…you are being silly.' Marco walked towards her and she backed away. She couldn't bear for him to touch her now. It was too raw…too painful to bear. 'Sarah had no right to say those things.'

'Has she spoilt your fun?' She flung the words at him bitterly.

'Charlie, stop it!' He reached out and caught her arm as she made to swing away from him.

'She had no right to say those things because they are not true.' He pulled her around and put a hand under her chin, forcing her to look up at him. 'I asked you to come to Italy with me because I needed your help in the office and I also thought we could have fun together. I wanted to spend time with you. I'll be honest that I was aware that the timing was convenient as far as a PR exercise is concerned…but that was just a bonus.'

Her heart was thundering painfully against her chest now and as he pulled her even closer she felt sure he would be able to feel it.

The words seemed to mock her…*have fun…convenient timing…PR bonus.*

'Just let me go, Marco…'

He ignored her. 'And we have had fun…haven't we?' His eyes were on her lips now.

Her heart twisted with painful need. And she hated herself for it.

With a supreme effort of will she wrenched herself away from him. 'Yes, it's been fun, Marco…but this is where it ends. From now on you'll have to find some other PR puppet to play games with.'

CHAPTER NINE

THEY were sitting side-by-side thirty-five thousand miles up in the air and they weren't talking.

It had been like this since they had left the villa to go to the TV station. Marco had tried to reason with her at first but she was in no mood to listen and somehow his words just seemed to make everything worse.

'You know you are being ridiculous,' he had muttered in the car. 'I don't know why you are blowing a conversation with Sarah Heart up out of all proportion.'

'Am I?'

She had seethed with hurt and anger.

'Yes, you are. I told you about Sarah's ideas up front.'

'You didn't tell me you were planning a PR exercise involving me behind my back!'

'It wasn't a PR exercise, it was a working weekend that was also supposed to be fun. And I didn't plan things behind your back. I made a passing remark to Sarah over dinner about how well we get on in the office and how you seem to be very in tune with my theories...and that's true...isn't it?'

The question was still causing unpleasant little ripples to spread throughout her body... She was accusing Marco of not being completely honest with her about his motivations this weekend—but she hadn't been completely honest with him either.

And there lay the crux of their problem. She was emotionally torn because she was in love with him. And he couldn't understand why she was so upset...because hey...it had just been a bit of fun anyway.

Charlie wondered if he had mentioned her at all during his interview on TV. She had sat waiting for him in the hospitality suite and had watched him on the monitor, but she hadn't understood a word because it was all in Italian. When the inevitable question about his personal life had arisen—what had he said?

Probably something along the lines of yes I'm dating my secretary. I feel very *comfortable* around her.

She glanced over at Marco, who had been flicking through the in-flight magazine, but he put it down now. He glanced over at her and their eyes met.

He looked so cool and collected and so damned handsome that instantly the raw pain of earlier sprang into ferocious life again. Being emotionally detached was too hard, she thought wretchedly. But she was going to have to try. And at the same time she hoped that he wasn't feeling quite so damn comfortable around her now.

'Have you calmed down now?' he asked quietly.

The cool enquiry just made her feel a hundred times worse. He was so damn cavalier!

When she thought about how she had opened up to him this weekend...tentatively trusted him...luxuriated in his warm embrace—and even dared hope he might return her feelings one day—it just made her want to either hit him or cry at her own stupidity.

'No, I haven't calmed down, Marco.' She was really pleased by how composed she sounded. There was no hint of turmoil in her voice. 'I don't appreciate being used in some cheap stunt.'

'Well, that certainly wasn't my intention!'

When she made no reply to that he frowned. 'Come on, Charlie, let's put this behind us and be friends again…hmm?'

Friends…the word grated mockingly inside her.

'I wouldn't have minded if you'd been honest with me,' she muttered, trying to ignore the little voice that was calling her a liar. 'I would have played the PR part to perfection…I mean, I understand the score, for heaven's sake.' She took a deep breath and forced herself to add, 'We were having a bit of light-hearted fun!'

'Exactly.' He looked at her with that teasing gleam in his eye that she knew so well. 'Look, I genuinely didn't think twice about Sarah's plans with the paparazzi. And I'm sorry you feel that I misled you. Let's just forget about it…hmm? And we can have lots more fun.'

He reached to take hold of her hand but she pulled away. If he touched her she didn't think she could maintain this air of indifference.

He was so arrogantly sure of himself! 'Yes, OK, we'll just forget about it,' she said stiffly. 'After all, we have to work together, don't we?' She swallowed hard and looked away from him out of the window.

If he wanted Ms Practicality, well, then, he could damn well have Ms Practicality in spades, she thought angrily. But she didn't want any more *fun* with him. It hurt too much.

The pilot announced that they would shortly be landing. Marco frowned and settled back in his seat. Obviously Charlie hadn't forgiven him! She was blowing the whole thing out of proportion…and he felt annoyed by the way she was being so cold towards him now. It wasn't a reaction he was used to where women were concerned.

He told himself to just forget about it. He'd apologised for any hurt feelings that he hadn't intended to cause. The weekend had been casual and the PR stunt had been Sarah's damn project, not his.

So why was he even thinking about it now? He had a meeting with Professor Hunt lined up for seven forty-five. And there were some extra notes he needed to deal with before then.

But he was furious with Sarah and his anger encroached on the businesslike thoughts. He had only just succeeded in getting Charlie to relax around him and now Sarah had ruined everything. How dared she say something so damn insensitive?

The last thing he wanted was to hurt Charlie… He glanced over at her. She was watching the TV screen on the seat in front of her, but he had the feeling she wasn't giving it her full attention. She looked so vulnerable sometimes that he wanted to reach out and touch her, take her into his arms and feel her melt against him in that incredible warm way of hers. She had been wonderful to be around…she was passionate, with a great sense of humour and she was great in bed. He was going to miss her tonight, in fact…

The plane touched down on the runway.

Marco pulled his attention away from Charlie and unfastened his seat belt. Outside the London afternoon looked grey and miserable, and there was a fine drizzle—the type that drenched you through without you realising it was happening.

As the aircraft came to a halt Marco stood up to get his briefcase and Charlie's hand luggage. 'Would you like to come back to my place for a coffee?' he asked casually as they walked together out into the terminal.

'No, thank you; I want to get home to Jack.' She smiled lightly.

'OK, well…you get your luggage and I'll go get the car and I'll see you outside in, say…twenty minutes?'

Charlie shook her head. 'I'll get a taxi, Marco. You may as well just go. There's no point you waiting around here when you have no luggage to collect.'

He frowned and for a moment his eyes raked over her face. She looked so young suddenly. 'But I want to see you home,' he insisted.

She desperately wanted to go with him and to forget the hurt that was insistently flowing through her. She longed to just lean in against him and kiss him…

But there was only so much pretence that she could handle and she had her pride. 'There's no point, Marco. You have an appointment, and don't forget, those notes you need are in a new file—'

'To hell with the files and the damn meeting, Charlie!' He sounded suddenly annoyed. 'Look, we've had a lovely weekend—why spoil it now?'

'I wasn't aware that I was spoiling anything.' She remained cool. 'Yes, it's been a nice weekend but we both have other commitments to get back to.'

What exactly was happening here? Marco wondered in agitation. He was usually the one making comments like this when a woman was coming on too strong!

He met her deep green guileless gaze. 'Yes, I suppose you are right…Professor Hunt is a bit of a stickler for time.' He forced himself to say the words and to sound positive and practical, but somehow for once in his life the feelings about work felt false.

Actually he couldn't have given a damn about Professor Hunt! He frowned. 'Are you sure I can't give you a lift?'

There was a moment's pause. Marco was barely aware of the crowds flowing around them as he looked at her. He wanted her to change her mind. He hated this sudden feeling between them that they were just strangers who had slept together…the warmth and passion of the weekend were too strong in his mind for him to be happy with that.

'Quite sure.'

'OK.' When she made no attempt to weaken he leaned closer…and then he saw her expression change. He saw a flicker of emotional intensity for just a moment. He smiled and then his lips crushed against hers in a passionately possessive way.

He felt a moment's resistance and then she kissed him back, her lips sweetly submissive and tantalising.

'See you in the office tomorrow,' he said with a smile as he stepped back.

She would forgive him, he thought with pleasure as he walked away.

This time tomorrow they would be working out the dates for her to join him in America.

Charlie opened her eyes and blinked against the early-morning sunlight. For just a moment she imagined that she was back in Italy with Marco and the feeling was joyous…then she stretched a hand out into the cool, empty side of the bed and the dark clouds of memory closed around her heart.

She groaned and buried her head in against the pillow. Sleep had been elusive last night, her mind going around in tortuous circles over her feelings for Marco. It hadn't solved anything because she still loved him and hated herself for the stupidity. How could you love someone when it was clear that they would never return your feelings?

The thought of facing him in the office today was unbearable and yet bitter-sweet all at the same time. How she was going to maintain a cool, professional distance she just didn't know.

Jack came running into the room. 'Morning, Mummy!' He leapt in beside her and she smiled and drew him close.

She had a little boy to take care of and responsibilities. She couldn't afford the time to be heartbroken, she told herself firmly. She needed this job with Marco and even if she could just stick it out for twelve months it would give her enough money to get herself back on track financially, pay for the things that needed doing around the house, pay her bills off…and then she could find some other position.

The sensible thought galvanised her into action and she

pushed back the bedcovers. She was just going to have to forget her feelings for Marco.

It was the usual Monday-morning rush to get out of the house. Once they were in the car Jack put her CD of love songs into the player and turned up the volume.

'I don't think I'm in the mood for that today, Jack.' She reached over and turned it off.

It was probably listening to music like that that had got her heart in this mess in the first place, she told herself fiercely. Marco was right about one thing: love *was* a dangerous emotion.

She dropped Jack off at school and headed for Marco's house with a heavy heart. It was the first time she had felt like this since she had started working for him. Usually she felt happy at the thought of spending the day with him…happy and excited. She had enjoyed being around him, enjoyed the little smiles he sent her way every now and then or the casual touch of his hand as it brushed against hers… Heck! Why hadn't she seen the fact that she was falling in love with him? she wondered in despair. It seemed so obvious now.

She parked her car next to Marco's and checked her appearance in the vanity mirror. Her hair was drawn back from her face and secured neatly in a pony-tail. Her make-up was applied with a careful skill to hide the shadows under her eyes and she had put a brighter shade of lipstick on today to cheer herself up. She would pass, she thought irately as she flicked the mirror shut. And she couldn't put this off any longer.

Taking a deep breath, she hurried into the house and up to the office. She could handle this, she told herself. She would be cool and practical and distant…

Her confidence dipped, however, as soon as she walked in. Marco was perched on the edge of her desk, flicking through the work calendar. It didn't help that he looked so handsome in a dark grey suit.

'Morning, Marco.' She tried to make her voice sound breezily indifferent.

He looked up and smiled at her and her heart missed a beat. Suddenly she was thinking about those mornings in Italy when he had wished her *buon giorno* and kissed her with steamy passion… Hastily she looked away and hung her jacket on the stand next to the door.

'So how are you today?' Marco asked quietly, his eyes following her movements.

'Fine, thanks; did your meeting with the professor go well?' It was the only thing she could think of to say that would help maintain a businesslike atmosphere. But inside she felt as if she was dying.

'Yes, thanks.'

To her consternation he made no attempt to move out of her way as she walked over towards her desk. Instead his eyes seemed to rake over her with sharp intensity.

'How was Jack last night?' he asked. 'I bet he was pleased to see you.'

'Yes, he was.' For a moment she remembered Jack hurtling across the room to hug her fiercely. She had wanted to cry as she had held him close. She wanted to cry again now. Her emotions were all over the place. She hadn't felt this level of hurt since the day her ex-husband walked out. And that angered her. She had promised herself that no man would ever make her feel like this again.

'Did he like his presents?'

'He loved them…especially the car, of course.' She tried not to think about that day in Florence and how they had laughed as they bought those toys together and then walked hand in hand. Which was all a damn set-up for the paparazzi, she reminded herself fiercely. Marco should mean nothing to her now, she thought severely…nothing. So why did she feel so broken inside when she looked over and met his eyes?

'Anyway, back to reality.' She smiled at him coolly and moved to go past so that she could sit at her desk.

He caught hold of her arm to stop her and the touch of his skin against hers made her senses instantly swim with desire. She flinched away, hating herself for the weakness.

Marco noticed and frowned. 'Listen, I was thinking we could have lunch together today,' he suggested softly. 'I've got to go over to St Agnes Hospital to give a second opinion on two referrals but I should be back around twelve.'

'I don't think lunch is a good idea, Marco.' Although her voice was calm, inside there were thunderous emotions racing…a big part of her wanted to say OK…that would be nice…

But she had to be strong, she thought. Because the more time she spent around Marco, the harder it would be to extract herself and switch off her emotions.

'Why not?' he asked calmly.

'Because…you know how I feel about mixing business with pleasure, it just doesn't work.'

'It worked when we were in Italy.'

The calm reply lashed at her emotions. 'No it didn't. And that was different, anyway; it was a…one-night stand.' She forced herself to say the words. That was all it had been, she reminded herself.

'As I recall, it was a little more than that.' He pulled her closer. She could smell the familiar tang of his cologne—evocative and warmly tantalising.

She still wanted him so much! The realisation killed her. How could she be so weak?

She pulled away. 'You and Sarah aren't cooking up another little photograph opportunity, are you?' she asked archly.

'No.' He frowned. 'I thought we'd agreed to put that behind us?'

'Yes…of course we have.' She chastised herself. Making

barbed comments wasn't a good idea. If Marco guessed how emotionally involved she was he would be horrified…maybe he would even tell Sarah Heart about it and the two of them would sit and discuss her and Sarah would smirk….

She switched her thoughts away from that. She was being ridiculous. Marco didn't know how she felt…and he never would. So her pride was intact, if nothing else.

'But we have a lot of work today, and I have letters to type.'

'Try to finish them by twelve o'clock. And then…' he leaned a little closer '…we could have some quality time…lunch and lovemaking….not necessarily in that order.' He whispered the words against her ear, his breath tickling against the sensitive area. 'I missed you last night.'

Her stomach flipped over with longing. She had missed him too…so much.

'I can't, Marco…really.' It took all her strength to keep her voice from trembling. Hastily she moved another step away.

'Why not?' He looked at her with a raised eyebrow. 'I've checked the calendar and both of our schedules this afternoon could be sidelined until tomorrow…'

'And then I'll be even further behind with things!' She went over to the filing cabinet to take some folders out. 'I want to keep things on a strictly business footing from now on.'

'As you know, I've no objection to keeping things business-like,' he said evenly, 'but today we could organise our time a little better and enjoy ourselves as well.'

'I don't think so.' Charlie shut the filing cabinet and went to sit behind her desk.

'You're still annoyed with me I take it?' Marco's tone was sardonic.

'No, of course not.' She found her reading-glasses and put them firmly on her nose. When he still didn't move and just continued to sit there with a wry look of sardonic disbelief in his eyes, she met his gaze firmly.

'Marco, I really enjoyed our weekend, but I don't think we should take things further. We've had our fun. I think it's time to move on.'

She could see the surprise in his dark eyes and felt wretched.

'You *are* still hung up about this PR business!'

'No I'm not!' She looked over at him calmly. 'I was mad at the time because you didn't tell me what your plans were up front. But now I'm just thinking in practical terms. And an affair with you is not what I need in my life right now.'

'So what do you need in your life right now?' he asked with a directness that made her frown.

'I have a four-year-old son, Marco. Stability is my main priority. Don't get me wrong, if I weren't a single mum I'd enjoy continuing our casual fling and playing a part in your PR plans. But under the circumstances I feel I need to be more circumspect about these things.'

'Well…I can understand that.' Although his voice was relaxed, he was looking at her through eyes that were slightly narrowed.

She was really relieved when the phone rang on her desk. 'Excuse me a moment.' She snatched it up as if it were a lifeline.

'Good morning, Professor Hunt,' she greeted Marco's colleague with cheerful enthusiasm. 'Yes, you've just caught him. Hold on.' She covered the mouthpiece. 'Shall I put him through to your private line?'

After a brief hesitation Marco nodded.

She returned to the phone with a false smile. 'I'm putting you through now, Professor,' she said, flicking a switch.

For a moment Marco didn't make any attempt to move and she thought he was going to ignore the call. Then suddenly he stood up. 'We'll continue our conversation later, Charlie.'

'I really have nothing more to say on the subject.'

She was pleased how together she sounded; weird really, when inside she was falling apart.

'Professor Hunt is waiting,' she reminded him firmly.

'Yes…I know.' His voice was dry. 'OK, Charlie, have it your way. I will, of course, still expect you to join me in America.'

Charlie felt a flicker of uncertainty. It was one thing keeping Marco at arms' length in the office but, as she knew from experience when they were away together, things got complicated. 'I told you to find someone else for your PR exercise.'

'And shall I find someone else as my PA as well?' he countered coolly. 'I thought we had agreed not to allow emotional issues to come before work?'

He watched her face flare with colour and for a moment he hated himself for pulling rank. But he wasn't about to let her slip away from him without a fight. 'The trip is purely business, Charlie,' he added more gently. 'But, as I said, we'll discuss this later.'

Charlie watched him head towards the inner office and close the door. Her heart was thundering out of control.

He was right, of course; she had just allowed personal feelings to come in the way of her job. But the simple truth was she couldn't go to America with him now even if it was strictly for business. Because, even knowing that she meant nothing to him, she still wanted him.

She bit down on her lip and despised herself for being so pathetic. Financially this job was a godsend and she was ruining it for herself.

Desperately she tried to think straight. But, no matter how calm and businesslike she tried to be, the mere thought of being alone with Marco in New York made her blood start to pound, confusing her senses with desire and trepidation.

The only solution was to get away from Marco as soon as possible. She was going to have to start job-hunting and fast.

CHAPTER TEN

CHARLIE had just stepped out of the shower when the front doorbell rang. She hurriedly reached for a towel and wrapped it around her wet hair before pulling a bath sheet around her. Karen had said she might call this morning if she had time. But by midday her friend still hadn't arrived, so Charlie had finished her housework and had started to get ready to go shopping.

'Jack, could you answer the door, please?' she called as she stepped out onto the landing.

There was no reply; Jack was playing with toys in the lounge.

Holding the towel tightly around her, she walked towards the stairs. She wanted to see Karen. They had spoken last week when Charlie had asked if she could find her another placement before the sale of her agency went through, which she had. But the downside was that the job was short-term and paid less.

She couldn't afford to drop her wages, so she'd had to refuse the offer.

Karen was coming to talk to her about it, and she hoped she wouldn't have to go into detail as to why she wanted to quit her job with Marco, as she found it too emotionally exhausting to explain. It had been hard enough working with him this week. The atmosphere in the office had been tense and she had been relieved to get out of there last night.

As Charlie started to go downstairs the doorbell rang again and Jack suddenly shot out of the lounge. 'I'll get it, Mum!' he said cheerily as he ran along the hallway.

'Oh, hi!' Charlie heard his cheerful greeting as he opened the door, and smiled. Jack was always pleased to see Karen. 'Mum's just got out of the shower.'

'Well, that was a bit of good timing.'

Charlie froze. It wasn't Karen—it was Marco's dulcet tones she could hear. And before she could stop him Jack was swinging the door wider to let him into the house. She looked down at herself in horror. All week she had maintained a well-groomed image with not a hair out of place. Somehow it had helped to know that at least she didn't look as if she was falling apart, even if she felt like it. Now Marco was going to catch her in a bath sheet with her hair in a towel!

'Actually, now isn't a good time,' she found herself calling out, trying to back up the stairs. 'I'm too busy to see anyone.'

He must have heard her, but he appeared at the bottom of the stairs anyway. She noticed the way his dark eyes swept boldly up over the long length of her legs and the curve of her figure. 'You look good in that towel.'

'Very funny,' she murmured. 'But, as you can see, I'm not in a fit state for visitors.'

The fact that he was his usual handsome and stylishly groomed self in a pair of chinos and a pale tan shirt didn't help her equilibrium at all.

'Don't worry about me. I like the turban look, by the way, it suits you—very exotic.'

She tried to ignore the seductive, teasing light in his eye, and fought to remain cool and reserved, but the truth was that her emotions were see-sawing wildly. There was a part of her that was so glad to see him…and she hated that. 'Was there something in particular you wanted, Marco?' She kept her tone cool.

'Yes, there is.' He folded his arms and leaned against the end of the banister rail. 'Are you coming down or shall I come up?'

'Neither,' she answered him quickly, her voice slightly unsteady. 'We're all right as we are.'

'You know that's not true.'

Something about the softness of his reply made her heart miss a beat.

'Which is why we need to talk,' he continued swiftly. 'And you can start by telling me exactly why you are job-hunting, because I think I have a right to know.'

Shock flooded through her. 'What makes you think I'm job-hunting?'

'Well, catching you looking through the situations-vacant column yesterday was a bit of a give-away,' he grated derisively.

She bit down on her lip, she'd only had a five-minute scan through the pages in her lunch break and he'd chosen that very moment to appear behind her with some papers he wanted her to file. She'd hoped he hadn't noticed, but she should have known better. Marco missed very little. 'I was just browsing,' she said defensively.

Marco was momentarily distracted by the fact that in her agitation she had allowed her towel to slip an inch, treating him to a provocative glimpse of her shapely curves. How was it that she could even look sexy in a bath towel? he wondered.

'So I take it you haven't found another job, then?' He forced himself to concentrate on the conversation.

'If I had, you would be the first to know.'

He raked a hand through the darkness of his hair. 'We really need to discuss this situation, Charlie.' His voice was reasoned. 'Go and get dressed and I'll take you to lunch.'

'No I will not!' She felt a flare of anger. 'You've no right to come barging around here on a Saturday, ordering me about.'

'You're right.' He held up his hands and his voice was gentle. 'But we need to sort this out, Charlie…and we haven't had a minute all week. I just feel that if we don't talk now you are going to walk away and I'm going to lose you.'

The words made her senses thunder unsteadily. Of course, he was only bothered about losing her in the office, she reminded herself fiercely and she hated herself for allowing that to hurt. 'Well, I wouldn't worry about it,' she retorted flippantly, 'because if I did leave you would no doubt find someone suitable to replace me very quickly.'

'But I don't want someone else.'

The quiet words wrenched at her emotions. So she was good at her job…but she wanted so much for him to need her on more than a business level. She looked away from him hurriedly as he suddenly swam in a mist before her eyes. Furious with herself, she blinked the tears back. She was being irrational.

Marco always thought in practical terms. That was part of who he was.

'Let me take you to lunch,' Marco said softly.

With determination she pulled herself together and looked back at him. 'I can't and anyway, I've no one to look after Jack.'

'That's OK—Jack is invited too.'

Charlie's eyes narrowed on him.

'There's a place down the road that is child-friendly apparently.'

'And why would you want to go somewhere like that?'

He looked at her with a serious light in his dark eyes. 'Because I think you'd like it.'

'Marco, I haven't found another job so there's really no need for you to take me out to lunch or be nice to my son. The crisis is averted…you still have your PA. And I really don't want to play games like that with you.'

'I think the time for games is over,' he cut across her firmly. 'And that's what I want to talk to you about.'

She frowned. What was he up to? she wondered.

'Just give me a few hours of your time, OK?' To her dismay he started to advance slowly up the stairs towards her.

She felt completely at a disadvantage and her heart was thundering at the purposeful glint in his eye.

Although he stopped on the stair beneath her, he was still a good head taller. 'By the way, your towel is slipping.' He reached and pulled it up a little for her.

She refused to blush. She didn't want to let him know how the touch of his hand made her long to go into his arms, and ache with a need that tore her in two.

Instead she held his gaze with determined green eyes, trying to ignore the prickles of awareness that were shooting through her. 'I don't think anything can be gained by us going out for lunch, Marco.'

'You know I think a lot of you, Charlie,' he said lightly. 'But on the negative side you do have a dreadful stubborn streak that can be very irritating.'

'You only think I'm stubborn because you can't twist me around your little finger.'

'And that's the other thing I like about you.' His fingers traced slowly over the side of her face. His eyes seemed to be on her lips. 'That no-nonsense attitude is very refreshing. You have the most incredibly lively mind.'

She stepped back from him. She didn't want to hear about how he admired her lively mind whilst he was caressing her like that—not when his touch was opening up a need inside her as wide as the Atlantic Ocean. 'Why don't you just say what it is you want to say, Marco? And then you can go.'

'Why would I do that and mess up a perfectly good opportunity for us to have lunch together…hmm?' He smiled. 'Plus I'm sure Jack would enjoy a trip out.'

'No he wouldn't…'

'Would we go in your car?' Jack's little voice from downstairs made them both look around in surprise. Charlie had thought he had gone back to playing with his toys once he had let Marco in.

He was standing quietly, watching them with avid interest.

'Yes, we'll go in my car, Jack.' Marco walked back downstairs and crouched down to speak to him. 'Would you like that?'

'That would be cool!' The little boy's eyes were alive with excitement now. 'Can we go, Mum? It would be great.'

Marco turned and looked at Charlie with a mocking gleam in his dark eyes.

Charlie tried not to be swayed by the fact that both of them were watching her closely.

'Please, Mum…please,' Jack said again.

Her eyes went from her son towards Marco.

'You know what they call this, don't you?' she told him wryly.

'No, what?' He straightened up.

'Emotional blackmail.'

'I'll take that as a yes, then,' he murmured with a smile.

It took Charlie ten minutes to dry her hair and throw jeans and a T-shirt on. She'd made no effort to try and look glamorous, and instead just tied back her hair and applied some lip-gloss.

Now she was sitting in the front seat of Marco's car, listening as her son chatted happily with him. Jack was asking about the car and Marco was giving him all the facts about it as if he were an adult. Charlie tried to relax back in the comfortable leather seat. She probably shouldn't have agreed to this but it did feel good being out with him again.

She watched the competent way he handled the powerful sports car through the country lanes. And for a moment her mind flicked back to that day in Italy when they had driven out towards Sienna and he had stopped the car and kissed her. Her eyes moved over his profile, remembering the tenderness and the steamy passion, and her heart missed a violent beat.

He looked over at her and caught her watching him and instantly she looked away. She shouldn't be thinking about things like that, she told herself furiously, because it didn't help and it didn't change anything. Marco's only concern was his work. He needed her around at the moment both in a PA capacity and a PR one, and he thought he could sweet-talk her into shelving any plans of leaving.

They turned through some high gateposts with the name Fogle Farm over them and pulled up outside an old country manor house.

'I think you'll like it here, Jack,' Marco said nonchalantly. 'They have a playground in the back and a pets' corner.'

Charlie glanced over at him as they stepped out of the car. 'So how did you find this place?'

'The internet recommends it as a place to bring children.'

Marco had obviously done some homework on this outing! 'You were very confident we were going to come out with you.'

'Quietly confident,' he corrected with a grin.

'Not really your kind of place, though, is it?' she couldn't resist adding as they walked around the side of the building and the sound of children shouting and laughing grew louder.

'Why do you say that?'

'Come on, Marco! Listen to it. It's not your sophisticated bachelor scene, is it?'

'You can get bored with sophisticated bachelor-type places.'

'Really?' She looked over at him sceptically.

'Yes, really.' There was a humorous spark in his dark eyes as they met hers. 'It's good to have variation in life.'

Marco took hold of Jack's hand as the child jumped up to walk along the edge of a low wall. 'We are going to have fun, aren't we, Jack?'

Jack nodded happily and Charlie noticed how he kept hold of Marco's hand as they followed the path around the house.

There was a huge play area around the back where a multitude of children were enjoying themselves, and before long Jack was dashing about, joining in the fun.

Although the sun was shining it was bitterly cold. Charlie huddled further into her jacket.

'You OK?' Marco came to stand back beside her.

'Yes.' She waved at Jack, who was on a merry-go-round now. 'Jack is having a lovely time.'

'I told you he'd enjoy it.'

'Hmm.' Charlie looked up at him wryly. 'The paparazzi aren't going to pounce out from behind a hedge at any moment, are they?'

The note of humour in her voice didn't fool Marco; he knew she was still bothered by Sarah's meddling. 'Is that why you are looking for a new job?'

'I was just idly glancing through the paper.'

'I don't believe that.'

'Well, as I said, you don't need to worry; I'm not going anywhere…not for a while anyway.' She shivered suddenly.

'You're cold!' Before she could stop him Marco had taken hold of her hands. He held them in the warmth of his for a moment and the touch of his skin against hers was electric. She swallowed hard as she looked up into his eyes. She wished with all her heart that she could switch off the intensity of her feelings for him, because it was so foolish…and it hurt so much.

'Why don't you go and sit inside?' He let her go and nodded towards the conservatory. 'There's a fire in there and you can watch Jack from the warmth. I'll stay out here to make sure he's OK.'

Charlie hesitated and then nodded. 'All right, thanks.'

Marco turned to watch Jack as he played. But his mind was still on Charlie.

When she had told him she wanted to keep their relationship on a strictly business footing he'd decided he would give her some space and then talk her around when they got to New York. It had been a shock to find her looking through the jobs column in the paper yesterday. He'd wanted to confront her immediately but had stopped himself.

Then he'd spent all last night mulling over it.

He couldn't let her go, and he didn't like that feeling. A long time ago he had prided himself on never making the same mistakes as his father.

But of course his need for Charlie was more pragmatic than illogical, he reassured himself firmly. Yes, he wanted her body…but she linked in with work…linked into all the ideas he had espoused in his book.

Jack ran over towards him. His coat had come unbuttoned and he was flushed with excitement. 'Can we go and see the animals now?'

'Yes, but I think you should do up that coat first.' Marco crouched down beside the child and fastened the buttons. 'That's better.'

To his surprise the child put his arms around his neck and gave him a quick hug. 'Thanks, Marco,' he said matter-of-factly before running off again.

As Marco watched him go he was suddenly reminded of days spent with his nieces and nephews. He'd thought of himself as a family man at heart once and had used to think that he wanted his own children one day, but somehow over the years other things had intervened and he'd lost sight of that part of himself.

Charlie was sitting in a booth by the warmth of the fire when Marco arrived back carrying Jack high on his shoulders. They were laughing, and both of them were glowing from the cold air outside.

She felt a jolt of surprise as she looked up at them. Marco seemed to be getting on very well with her son! But then anyone could get on with a child for a short space of time she assured herself as she watched him put Jack down. It didn't mean anything special.

'Mum, I saw some black potbelly pigs.'

'Did you, darling? That's wonderful. What else did you do?'

'Marco pushed me really high on the swings.'

'Did he? That's great.' Charlie reached to help Jack take his coat off.

She noticed that Marco only had to glance in the waitress's direction and she came over to take their order. What was it about him that had everyone instantly running to please him? she wondered. It irritated her, and it irritated her even more that she felt warm inside as she met his eyes.

Why couldn't she shut out these feelings for him? she wondered frantically.

'Mum, can I go over there?' Jack pointed towards the next room, where other children were in an indoor play area.

Charlie hesitated. 'OK, but you've got to come back as soon as your lunch arrives.'

'He's a great kid,' Marco said with a smile as he watched him run off. 'His dad is missing out, not seeing him.'

The words prickled through Charlie's emotions. 'What are you playing at, Marco?' she asked quietly. 'I know you don't want to lose me as your PA but taking me out and pretending to have an interest in Jack—'

'I'm not pretending anything!' He met her eyes steadily. 'I meant every word.'

He sounded so sincere that he made her feel almost guilty for daring to say such a thing. Then he smiled at her across the table and she felt her defences start to melt away.

Hurriedly she glanced away from him and tried to compose herself. Marco was a charmer with an eye to the main chance, she reminded herself.

'I've been thinking about what you said when you ended things between us the other day,' he said suddenly.

She glanced back at him with a frown.

'About how you have to consider the effect a casual relationship could have on Jack,' he continued smoothly. 'And how you have to give him stability. I admire you for that. It must be hard bearing all the responsibility for bringing up a child single-handedly.'

'I manage very well.' She met his gaze steadily. 'Why are you trying to charm me?'

'Do you have to be so suspicious? Look, before you say anything more, just hear me out. Of course I don't want to lose you as my PA but this goes deeper.' His voice lowered and was suddenly very emphatic. 'The thing is, I've realised since coming back from Italy that I don't want to lose you *at all.* I like having you in my life.'

Charlie felt her heart starting to thump painfully against her chest. She had wanted desperately to hear him say something like this but now that it was actually happening she couldn't quite believe it.

He noticed the guarded light in her green eyes.

'I know you've been through a painful divorce and you are cautious about relationships. And I can understand where you are coming from. As you know, I'm wary myself.'

'I had noticed,' she said lightly and he smiled.

'And that's one of the reasons I think we are good together. Neither of us are taken in by glib, meaningless words. We are both very down-to-earth with our expectations and are on a certain wavelength.'

Charlie felt herself starting to tense up; any minute now he was going to tell her he felt *comfortable* around her! 'I don't know if we are *that* similar, Marco…' she murmured uneasily.

'Of course we are. Didn't you tell me once when you were internet-dating that you were looking to meet someone who would fulfil a certain criteria as a good partner?'

'Companionship.' Charlie said the word numbly. 'I think

that was the word I used.' She remembered the conversation clearly and recalled her lie with excruciating intensity.

'You were very realistic.' Marco nodded. 'And the more I think about it the more I realise what a good team you and I would make.'

'A good team?' Her voice didn't sound as if it belonged to her. She felt slightly dazed by all of this. 'What exactly do you mean by that?'

He looked over at her with a serious expression in his dark eyes. 'I mean that instead of ending our relationship we should allow it to develop into something more serious. I am talking about a partnership.' He leaned a little closer across the table. 'I want you to move in with me, Charlie.'

Charlie stared at him in shock. Silence stretched in a long, tense moment. She wasn't aware that her hands were clenched and her nails were cutting into her skin until Marco reached across to take both hands in his. He smoothed out her fingers and held them gently.

'So what do you say?' he asked softly.

Charlie pulled away from him abruptly. She couldn't allow herself to be swayed by the feelings that his touch generated and she couldn't afford to ignore the facts. Marco had asked her to move in with him and that was exciting and wonderful and her heart had leapt for a moment when he said the words. But there was one little word missing from the equation. And that was love.

But of course he hadn't mentioned that word because he wasn't in love with her, she reminded herself drily. You only had to listen to his reasoning to know that to him the emotion was of little importance, and much more vital was the fact that he thought they were suited in practical terms, that they would make *a good team*.

'I realise I've sprung this on you and it is a big step...but I'm confident that it will work,' Marco continued when she said nothing.

How could it work when love would never be of secondary importance to her? The knowledge swept through her painfully.

'Well, I'm sorry, Marco, but I'm not.' She swallowed hard on a knot that was forming in her throat. 'The answer has to be no.'

He looked rattled for a moment. 'Charlie, think about it! You and I get on brilliantly. For a start we work well together and that says a lot for a relationship's chances—'

'You are starting to sound like your book.' She cut across him derisively. She didn't want to hear all the calm, practical reasons why they would be good together—he was asking her to move in with him, for heaven's sake! At the very least she wanted *some* sentiment, although the fact that she was being totally unrealistic even thinking like that made her all the more angry with herself and him. 'Next you will be telling me not to allow emotion to influence my decision,' she muttered.

'Not a bad piece of advice,' he said calmly. 'You should always allow facts to influence decisions…nothing else.'

'And what about the fact that this could be another one of your damn publicity stunts?' she flared.

'Is that why you are saying no?' He relaxed suddenly and his expression softened. 'Hell, Charlie…I admit you are a tremendous plus point when it comes to handling questions from the media but asking you to move in is no mere stunt. I wouldn't do that!'

The gentleness of his tone made her reactions swing wildly from angry to tearful. She forced herself not to give in to that weakness, and instead to remember how he had discussed her in cool, clinical terms with Sarah Heart. 'Wouldn't you?' She raised her chin a little higher. 'I'm not so sure.'

'Well, I assure you that is not the case,' he said firmly. 'I am who I am, Charlie. And if I sound like my book it's because I believe in the theories. And I'm asking you to move in because I think that you and I will work.'

'So I'm a kind of test case now?' she observed mockingly. 'How romantic!' She couldn't help the sudden emotional outburst.

'Charlie!' He frowned. 'You are being ridiculous now! The fact is that we get on. We enjoyed Italy, didn't we? It was steamy and passionate. We are sexually compatible.' The huskily compelling tone of his voice made her senses blur. 'There is no doubt about that.'

He was right, there was no doubt about that. But to him it was just sex and to her it meant a hell of a lot more.

'Why don't we just give things a try?' he continued smoothly. 'Move in with me and we'll test the waters. What's the worst that can happen?'

She took a deep breath and sat back. The worst that could happen was that she would get her fragile heart well and truly smashed to pieces. And she knew what that was like all too well.

'I can't, Marco.' The reminder served to make her voice calm and steady now. 'I have my son to consider. I can't just move in and casually test things out with you. My responsibilities won't allow for that—'

'I think you are hiding behind your responsibilities.'

'I'm not hiding behind anything,' she said firmly. 'And may I remind you that a few moments ago you were admiring me for taking my responsibilities so seriously?'

'I do admire you for that, but right at this moment you are hiding behind them.'

The obdurate certainty in his tone annoyed her. 'Have you stopped to consider for one moment what it would be like having a four-year-old around? You are a confirmed bachelor, for heaven's sake!'

'Of course I've considered it! You and Jack are a package deal and that is not a problem because I like Jack.'

'You don't even know Jack!'

'I know that he is a lovely little boy who could benefit from having a father figure around.'

'Don't you dare bring that into the equation!' She glared at him and felt tears suddenly prickling behind her eyelashes. Angrily she blinked them away.

'It's true though, isn't it?' He held her gaze steadily. 'You told me that yourself.'

'I meant it would be nice to have someone who will be around for him. Not someone who has decided he wants to play at fatherhood on a whim.'

'This isn't a whim, Charlie. I would have thought you knew me better than that. I would like to be there for you and Jack. I'm offering you a stable, secure environment for your child. All I ask in return is that you are there for me—'

'That I share your bed, you mean.'

'But of course.' He smiled and his eyes held hers with bold emphasis. 'I'll want you on a regular basis. That goes without saying.'

She tried to ignore the sudden flare of heat inside her at those teasingly provocative words and cut across him coolly. 'So that you can prove your theory that love is unnecessary for a successful relationship.'

'So that I can prove that I'm right and we are compatible for a long-term partnership,' he corrected her with a frown.

The door opened behind them and a blast of cold air rushed into the conservatory as a crowd of people came in.

Charlie was glad of the distraction and the opportunity to compose herself. She watched the fire flicker dangerously low as the draught caught it and then flame into roaring life again as the door closed. A bit like her emotions, she thought sardonically.

'It's getting busy in here,' Marco reflected. 'Hardly the best place for this conversation.' He looked back at her, taking in the pallor of her skin and the steel-like determination as she raised her chin and met his gaze.

He hadn't meant to talk to her about all this in here; he'd been going to wait until later. And he now had a feeling he had pressed her too hard. If he wasn't careful she might rebel and go in the opposite direction. He needed to take a more softly-softly approach or he was going to lose her.

'Just give the idea some thought…OK?' he asked calmly. 'We can discuss it more when we get back to your place.'

'Actually I've got my friend Karen coming round,' Charlie said dismissively, 'so that won't be possible.'

He looked at her with a raised eyebrow. 'But you will give it some thought?'

For a few heartbeats she didn't answer. She *couldn't* answer, because she knew the correct response should still have been no.

How could she move in with Marco and share his bed— share his life—knowing that the whole relationship was based on the premise of a lie…*her lie*. Not only that, but she'd always have the knowledge that he didn't love her…maybe would never love her.

Could she really live with that?

CHAPTER ELEVEN

'Is CHARLIE going to go to America with you next week?' Sarah Heart asked, popping the question casually into the conversation as Marco stood up to leave her office.

'I don't know yet.' Marco's reply was terse. He glanced across at Sarah and could see she was dying to ask further questions but didn't dare. Probably because he had told her in no uncertain terms that he didn't like the way she had spoken to Charlie on the phone in Italy. And it was now a raw subject.

'Time is moving on, Marco,' she said instead, her tone cautious.

'Yes, I'm well aware of that.' Marco picked up his briefcase from her desk. It was just over a week since he had asked Charlie to move in with him and she still hadn't given him her answer.

'You've got two tickets for the literary dinner at the Plaza Pendinia in New York. Do you think she will join you there?'

'I've told you, I don't know. Just leave the subject alone, Sarah.'

She shrugged and looked momentarily annoyed. 'I'm just trying to do my job. But…you know your own business, I suppose.'

He met her gaze firmly. Sarah was seriously starting to irritate him. He'd been tempted to fire her after the debacle of the way she had spoken to Charlie in Italy. Only the fact that his tour in America was imminent and the timing was wrong had held him back. 'Yes, I do. And don't forget that!' There was an underlying steel-like warning in the words. 'You work for me, not the other way around, Sarah.'

'Yes, of course!' Sarah backed down immediately. 'Don't let's fall out. You know I only have your best interests at heart!'

'Just don't overstep the line, OK?' he said heavily.

'Scouts' honour!' she said with a gleam of mischief in her eyes.

He smiled. 'You are impossible.'

'I know!' She batted long, dark eyelashes and looked at him coyly. 'Look, I have a few meetings set up in NY for next week and I'll probably attend the dinner at the Plaza myself. So if you want I can accompany you that evening. I don't mind playing the part of your lover for a while. I can create some great spin out of it for you.'

'Thanks for the offer, Sarah!' Marco laughed. 'But I don't think it's such a good idea.'

'I don't see why. I think we'd be quite believable as a couple. You can use me in your interviews…' She lowered her voice huskily. 'In fact, you can use me any way you want,' she added playfully.

'You are my agent, Sarah. Let's keep it that way.' Marco shook his head and turned away towards the door. 'Besides my name is already linked with Charlie.'

'That's in the European papers—'

'Sarah, I've said no.'

'You are losing your sense of humour these days,' she muttered in annoyance and then hurried after him as he walked towards the lift.

She was probably right, Marco acknowledged drily. He knew he was on a short fuse. It was all this waiting around for an answer from Charlie. He was trying to take things slowly but he wasn't a patient man at the best of times. He'd tried a little old-fashioned courtship, by sending her flowers, and he'd behaved like a total gentleman…but it was getting him precisely nowhere. The only plus point was that he was getting to know and like Jack a lot. Which was just as well because every time he called at Charlie's house he had ended up spending more time with him than he had alone with her.

He wasn't used to being fobbed off where a woman was concerned. The suspense was killing him; and yet at the same time he was firmly convinced that she was worth waiting for. He wondered suddenly if she had been deliberately testing him to see how he got on with her son…?

'Marco?'

As they stepped out of the lift he realised Sarah was speaking about an interview in LA that she was still setting up.

'Sorry. I've got things on my mind at the moment, Sarah,' he told her distractedly. 'I'll phone you to get the last-minute details. I'm flying to Edinburgh for a conference later tonight. I'll be there for five days.'

Sarah frowned. 'Yes, I'd forgotten.'

Marco turned to look at her. 'I know this tour in the States is important, Sarah. But the most important thing to me is my work.'

'I know that, Marco.'

'Good; well, just keep that in mind when you are handling the PR, OK?'

'Don't worry.' She smiled and then stood on tiptoe to kiss him on the cheek. 'I'm here to assist you in any way I can.'

'That's good to know,' he said wryly as he turned away.

'And don't forget my offer to be the ideal prototype partner in the US is always open.'

'I'm hoping the position is already filled.' He looked back at her. 'And on the subject of Charlie, try to use some discretion.'

As he stepped out onto the street Marco hailed a taxi and climbed in. He was glad Sarah had no inkling that he had asked Charlie to move in with him. If she had she would be working out a spin on it for the papers already.

He supposed that was what made her so good at her job. But he didn't like it. He just hoped he hadn't made a mistake in not firing her.

The traffic going out of London was gridlocked. Marco glanced at his watch. Charlie would have shut the office and gone home if this didn't clear soon. Damn! He had been hoping he would catch her before she left. He intended to get an answer from her before he set off for Edinburgh. The time for playing this softly-softly game with her was over.

Flicking open his phone, he dialled the office number. She answered after the first ring.

'Dr Delmari's office.'

Her breezy, efficient tone made him smile. 'Hi, it's me,' he said, settling back against the seat. 'How are things with you?'

He listened as she started to give him a run-down on the office. He'd hardly been in today but by the sounds of things she had kept everything running smoothly.

'How did your meetings go?' she asked when she had run out of the day's events.

'Fine. All finished. I'm caught up in traffic. I'll be at least another hour.'

'OK; well, don't worry—I'll lock up here—'

'No, you are going to have to wait for me,' he cut across her firmly. 'We have things to sort out before I go to Edinburgh.'

'Can it wait?'

Her brisk tone had gone now and he could hear the caution creeping in.

'No, Charlie, it can't.' He hung up.

Charlie went down to Marco's kitchen and switched the kettle on. There wasn't much else to do. She had finished all the filing and had even made a start on tomorrow's jobs.

As she waited she glanced around at the kitchen with new eyes. Although she had been in here a hundred times before, she had never paid much attention to her surroundings other than to admire the expensive fittings, the pale ash cupboards and the black granite worktops. Now she was looking at it all with new eyes.

She was trying to picture herself and Jack here and it was surprisingly easy. If she said yes to Marco they would sit as a family at the kitchen table, laughing and talking… She could even see Marco and Jack playing football in the garden and racing the remote-control cars out on the patio. There was no doubt that the two liked each other. She had watched them together over these last couple of weeks and there was an easy rapport between them that couldn't be faked.

In fact, Marco's patience with Jack had completely surprised her. For an inveterate bachelor he was remarkably good with children.

Not that that should make any difference to her answer. It was a definite plus that Jack and Marco got on but she couldn't say yes just because of that.

But there were other positive points in favour of saying yes, a little voice reminded her unequivocally. For a start there was the fact that she wanted to go back into Marco's arms. Every night she lay in bed and she ached for him.

She had felt lonely after Greg had left her—in fact, she had thought she was heartbroken, but it was nothing to the gaping great chasm she had inside her now.

It didn't matter how many times she told herself that she should have more self-respect than to love a man who didn't return the feelings. She still wanted him, and she still loved him.

And that was why her answer had to be no, she reminded herself fiercely as she spooned some coffee into a pot. She couldn't live a lie, pretending to be emotionally detached, pretending she didn't care that Marco saw her in terms of practicalities rather than love. She should never have weakened and said she'd think about it. Because when she did get the strength to say no again he'd probably think she had been stringing him along. But she hadn't, she just couldn't bring herself to say the word and make the sensible choice.

She could tell recently that he was becoming impatient. And by the tone of his voice on the phone just now it sounded as if they had reached crunch point. She could have tried to stall him by telling him she had to get home for Jack, but the truth was that Jack was sleeping over at Karen's house tonight, as it was her son's birthday party. And anyway she couldn't in all conscience put this off any longer.

The sound of the front door opening jarred on her senses like a starter gun. This was it; there was no more room for prevarication. Sorry, Marco…she practised the words in her head. The answer is still no…

'I'm in the kitchen, Marco,' she called out as she heard him cross the hall. She heard his footsteps change direction and stop in the doorway. She could feel his eyes on her back.

'I'd finished everything upstairs so I thought I'd make a drink. Would you like one?' So much for not prevaricating, she thought deprecatingly.

'No, thanks.' His voice was brusque.

She didn't look around, and just continued to pour the boiling water over the coffee grains. The rich aroma suddenly reminded her of mornings in Italy and the heat of their passion. *Don't think about that,* she warned herself sternly.

He walked towards her and then reached across to put an envelope down on the counter beside her.

'What's that?' she asked warily.

'Air tickets: I booked you a flight from Heathrow to JFK on the 20th of the month.'

She looked down at the envelope and made no attempt to pick it up or to move.

'I want you there in your capacity as my PA. But I also want you there as my partner.'

He put a hand on her shoulder and turned her firmly to face him. And suddenly she was very close to him…too close, in fact. His body was just a whisper from hers.

She looked up at him and wanted to drown in the darkness of his eyes.

'I've waited long enough for your answer. I need to know now.' He reached and touched her face. The whisper-soft caress made her senses soar. 'Will you move in with me?'

'I think it's too big a step…too great a risk.' She tried to focus on the practicalities of the situation, just as he had advised. 'I've worked very hard to be independent and if I sell my house and things go wrong with you—'

'Don't sell it.' He cut across her decisively. 'Hold on to it and rent it out.'

'So if it doesn't work out between us I just move back in as if nothing has happened?' Her voice held an edge of derision.

'It's just a security net.' Marco shrugged. 'I'm confident you won't need it. Things will work out,' he said calmly.

'I don't know how you can be so sure. You lived with someone once before…and that didn't work out did it—'

'That was different,' he said dismissively.

'How was it different?' She looked up at him and willed him to give her one shred of evidence that he might learn to love her the way she loved him. All this businesslike discussion when he was so close was just tearing her apart. She longed for some emotion…some wild declaration of feelings.

'Some relationships aren't meant to progress beyond an affair. But you and I have something real…something solid to build on.' His eyes moved over her countenance searchingly.

It should have been enough but it wasn't. She took a deep, shuddering breath. 'Marco—'

'I want you, Charlie…' he murmured huskily.

Her heart bounced unsteadily against her chest at the sudden words.

God, she wanted him too. Did it really matter that he was talking in practicalities to her? Greg had given her all the words of love in the world and they hadn't meant a thing in the end.

Tears prickled behind her eyes.

'OK, I'll join you in the States but—' She had been going to say that they could talk after that about moving in together.

His lips on hers abruptly silenced the words. At first the kiss was gently searching, and then suddenly it became hungrily possessive, plundering her softness with brutal, forceful intensity.

'No more prevarication, Charlie…you'll join me in the States on my terms and then on my return you will join me here in this house and in my bed.'

His mood was dangerously forceful, but the really frightening part was that she started to yield to him instantly.

'Maybe…we could give things a try…' Her arms wound up and around his neck.

'That's better…' There was a smug satisfaction in his tone at her acquiescence. 'I don't know how I've waited this long for you…' He murmured the words huskily against her lips. 'You've been playing a very dangerous game with me, Charlie…'

'I don't play games.' She felt almost delirious with need as he trailed fiercely heated kisses down her neck. 'I've made one mistake in my life and I'm just scared of making another.'

He pulled away from her a little and looked into her eyes. 'I know you've been badly hurt in the past. And perhaps deep down you believe that you are still a little in love with your ex.' He put a finger on her lips, silencing her protests. 'It doesn't matter…your ex-husband is in the past, Charlie, and I know you are sensible enough to realise those feelings aren't reliable. What we have is real…it's sensible and it will work.'

The word *sensible* might have jarred on her except for the

way he was looking at her and the tone of his voice. She was aware that his hands were high around her waist and that his thumbs were stroking the edge of her bra.

'Now…' his hands moved and he swiftly started to unfasten the buttons on her blouse '…I've got four hours to kill before heading to the airport. Let's seal the deal and go to bed.'

'You are totally outrageous, Marco…' She trailed off as he leaned forward and kissed her with a slow, seductive passion that rocked her world completely.

'Outrageously hungry for you…' He growled the words close to her ear.

The jacket of her suit fell to the floor and then her skirt was being unzipped before it joined her jacket. Her bra was quickly removed as she felt his hot lips move down towards her soft curves.

Charlie raked her fingers through the darkness of his hair. She was beyond any reasonable, sensible thoughts now. All she could do was give in wholeheartedly to the feelings of desire that were suddenly raging out of control inside her.

Sex with Marco was incredibly enjoyable and satisfying but also completely exhausting, Charlie thought with a smile as she lay in his arms.

She remembered how things had got completely out of control between them in the kitchen. He had ripped her clothes off whilst kissing her and touching her with an expertise in seduction that blew her mind. The very memory made her blush. She had pictured many things in that kitchen but she hadn't pictured herself naked, with Marco taking pleasure in her against the counter-tops!

It had been crazy and wild and wonderful and then he had brought her upstairs to his bedroom and had taken her all over again. She was still breathless and still gathering her senses.

'I'm going to have to go. I haven't packed and I've got to

be at the airport in an hour.' He gave her a swift kiss on the forehead before pulling away from her.

She watched as he walked over towards his wardrobes and opened them. He was completely unselfconscious about his nakedness, she noticed. Although it was no wonder really because he had an incredibly perfect body. It made her marvel all over again that Marco wanted her. *He really wanted her.* It didn't matter to him that her body wasn't perfect or that she wasn't a model-like beauty. He liked her the way she was.

The knowledge made her glow inside or maybe that was just the after-effects of some very stimulating lovemaking, she thought with a smile.

Marco took out a suit and hung it on the side of the door. Then he went into the *en suite* bathroom.

Charlie took the opportunity to get out of bed and retrieve her clothes that were scattered on the floor. She had just put on her underwear when he appeared back in the room, a towel wrapped around his waist.

She felt shy suddenly as his eyes swept over her figure, which was absurd, given the circumstances.

'Do you have to go and pick up Jack?' he asked casually.

'No, he's at my friend's house for the night.' She reached for her blouse and quickly put it on.

'So we could have had the night together if I wasn't rushing off?'

She nodded.

'That's unfortunate.' He shook his head. 'This conference couldn't have come at a worse time.'

'Never mind, we will see each other when you get back.'

'Unfortunately I'll be on a tight schedule when I get back. I have a meeting with Dr Sinclair at the hospital to hand over my list of patients for the two months I'm away. And after that I've got to catch a midnight flight to LA.'

Charlie felt a flicker of disappointment, as she hadn't

realised he was leaving for the States so soon. 'I thought you were leaving a few days after you got back from Edinburgh?'

'Sarah has changed the schedule to fit in an extra interview on the Ed Johnson show.'

'That's a very popular programme.' Charlie reached for her skirt and stepped into it.

'Yes, prime-time stuff, so a great start to the tour. Sarah can be irritating but she knows what she's doing.'

Charlie didn't even want to think about Sarah, never mind talk about her.

'But it means I'm going to need you to reschedule a lot of my appointments for the extra days I'm away,' Marco continued lightly.

'Don't worry, I'll sort things out.' She looked away from him. All this talk of business straight after their lovemaking was disconcerting. 'We'll catch up when I join you in New York,' she added softly.

'I'm so glad I asked you to move in with me.' He smiled. 'Because you and I are going to get along just fine, Charlie...do you know that?'

'I hope so.' There it was again...that practical tone in his voice that flayed at her emotions. She tried not to think about it too deeply and instead started to tidy her hair, brushing it back from her face with her fingers.

'I know so...' he walked back towards her '...because you are just what I need. Reliable, uncomplicated and perfect in every way.'

That sounded like an endorsement for the perfect PA, not a live-in lover.

For a moment she couldn't bear to look up at him because the ache inside her was suddenly heavy and deep. She loved him so much and longed for him to return her feelings.

The need was so intense that it flayed her and that in turn made her angry.

What did she expect? she asked herself furiously. This was Marco. He was a warm and passionate lover but not one for flowery sentiment. Practicalities came first; she would have to accept that if she wanted to make their relationship work.

He put a hand under her chin and tipped her face upwards, his eyes moving searchingly over her countenance.

She tried to veil her feelings and look at him with self-assurance. He smiled as he noted the proud way she held his gaze. Then he bent and kissed her softly on the lips, making the ache intensify, tinged with sweet, searing desire.

She was very glad that he didn't look into her eyes again as he pulled away…because she was sure he would have seen a glimpse of her pain and that would have been too much to bear.

He turned to open a bedside drawer. 'I've got a spare front-door key in here somewhere…ah, yes, here it is. You may as well start moving some of your belongings in whilst I'm away.'

Marco held the key out towards her.

She didn't take it immediately. 'What about work?' she asked uncertainly.

'What about it?' He looked at her wryly. 'I was hoping we'd continue as we are…for now anyway. But don't worry I'll be a very flexible boss,' he added teasingly.

When she still didn't take the key he reached out for her hand and pressed it into her palm. 'Now…that's enough talk about work. We can sort details like that out at any time.'

'Yes…I suppose we can.' Her hand closed over the key. She was going to do this. Because she wanted Marco…wanted him with all her heart. And maybe one day he would return her feelings. Maybe he just needed to learn how to trust her, and if she was patient everything would come right…

He smiled. 'So how about going back to bed?'

The sudden huskily sexual request took her by surprise. 'What about your flight?'

'I'll take a later one.' He leaned closer and kissed her and it was so incredibly possessive that she instantly melted against him. 'We've got some more catching up to do before I go anywhere,' he growled.

CHAPTER TWELVE

THE stretched limousine turned on to Fifth Avenue and Charlie looked out at the familiar names…the Rockefeller Centre, Saks, Tiffany's, Cartier. She felt as if she had been beamed down into a film set and that this wasn't real somehow.

The lights of the city glittered diamond-bright against the velvet darkness of the night and the whole place seemed to pulsate with life and energy.

Excitement curled inside her. She was finally here in New York and Marco was waiting for her at the hotel.

He hadn't been able to meet her at the airport because of a book-signing session, and although she had told him she would take a cab into the city he had insisted on sending a limo for her.

Charlie couldn't wait to see him. It was two long weeks since he had left London and she hadn't thought it was possible to miss someone this much. Just the sound of his voice on the phone had made her throb inside. She longed to be held in his arms.

The limousine pulled to a halt in front of an impressive hotel. A doorman hurried down the red-carpeted steps and opened her door.

She stepped out onto the street and was immediately engulfed by noise. The sound of the traffic and the urgent blare of a siren seemed to reverberate between the tall buildings.

By contrast the inside of the hotel was tranquil, with a pianist in the centre of the lobby playing classical music on a gold baby-grand piano. Fresh flowers perfumed the air and the blue and gold décor was elegantly sophisticated.

She walked across the thickly carpeted foyer towards the reception area.

'Ah, Ms Hopkirk, Dr Delmari has left a message for you.' The receptionist handed her an envelope from one of the pigeonholes as she signed the register. 'You are in suite 200 on the top floor. I'll arrange for someone to bring your luggage up. Have a pleasant stay.' He slid a key card across to her.

Charlie opened the envelope as she walked towards the lifts. Inside there was a short note in Marco's flowing handwriting.

Hi Darling,

I'm going to be longer than I thought. It's a damn nuisance but it can't be helped. Don't forget we are to attend the literary dinner at the Plaza Pendinia tonight and we have to be there by eight. Hope you feel up to it after your long flight.

Looking forward to seeing you,

Marco

Charlie felt a dart of disappointment. She knew that they would only have a few short hours alone together before having to go to this dinner and she had hoped to spend every spare minute in his arms. It looked as though that wasn't going to happen. She crumpled the note and tossed it into a waste bin. It couldn't be helped, she told herself firmly, and at least it would give her a chance to freshen up and make herself more presentable before seeing him.

The lift doors opened on the top floor and she walked down towards the suite. It was spectacularly elegant inside. There

was a lounge area and then the biggest double bed Charlie had
ever seen in her life. There was also a magnificent bouquet of
flowers for her on the table, and next to it Marco had scribbled
on a gift tag, *I've missed you.*

Charlie smiled. Marco may not believe in romance but he
was very thoughtful. She just wished he had put the word *love*
somewhere on the card. Though as soon as the thought crossed
her mind she dismissed it. She had told herself she wasn't
going to dwell on things like that. It was enough that Marco
wanted her, and maybe one day his feelings would deepen.

He had certainly phoned her enough times during the fort-
night he'd been away. And, although a lot of the conversation
had centred on business-related issues, a fair amount had also
centred on the fact that she was going to move into his house.
It had been exciting talking about it; Marco had given her free
rein to arrange things and had told her to choose whatever room
she wanted for Jack. She hadn't moved any of her belongings
in yet, though, it hadn't seemed right with him not being there.
But at least he had made it clear that he wanted her to treat his
house as home, and just wanted her to be happy.

That solicitous, caring manner was enough for now, she
assured herself. Plus there was the fact that, sexually-speaking,
their relationship was so hot it was on fire. She wished he
would hurry and get back from this damn book-signing...

The porter arrived with her luggage and she tipped him and
then unpacked. She had bought a new dress for tonight and she
hung it up in the *en suite* bathroom so that the steam from her
shower would get rid of any creases.

Then she stripped off and turned on the shower. She didn't
feel too bad after her journey because Marco had booked her
a first-class air ticket and she had been pampered all the way.
But it was lovely to stand under the hot, refreshing jet of water
and get rid of the stale feeling of travel.

She dried her hair and left it loose in soft waves around her face. Then she glanced at her watch. There was less than an hour now before they had to be at the dinner. So she started to put on her make-up and get ready.

Charlie was sitting in the lounge, flicking through the TV stations, when she heard the front door open and Marco walked in.

Her heart caught in her chest as she saw him. He looked so dynamically handsome that it was hard to believe he was her lover, or that this was for real. She felt suddenly shy, as she had gone to a lot of trouble with her appearance for tonight and she hoped he liked the way she looked.

'Sorry, honey—that was more of a marathon than I could ever have imagined.' He tossed the key card down on the side and walked towards her. 'Did you have a good flight?'

He stopped in his tracks as she stood up. 'God, you look amazing!' His eyes moved over her appraisingly.

His wolf-whistle and the way he was almost undressing her with his dark eyes made her blush. 'Thanks,' she smiled at him. She knew the dress was fantastic. The material was pale blue silk and its cut flattered her figure to perfection, emphasising her slender waist and her curves before falling to the floor in straight, sophisticated lines.

'You said to get something special to wear so I did. I hope it's suitable.'

'It's more than suitable! The only problem is I don't want to take you out now, I want to take you to bed,' he said huskily as he came a little closer.

'Well, unfortunately we don't have time for that.'

He trailed one finger down over the smooth, creamy perfection of her face, his eyes on the softness of her lips. 'I've missed you…'

'I missed you too.' Her heart missed several beats as he took her into his arms and kissed her.

At first the kiss was tenderly sensual but it quickly turned intensely possessive. She felt his hands on her body in a firm caress and sexual hunger tore through her like a searing, white-hot heat.

The phone on the table rang and he pulled back from her with a smile of regret. 'Do you mind if I get that? It might be important.'

'No...of course not.' She sat back down to wait for him. It didn't matter, she told herself. They would have all night together after this dinner and then three whole days and nights before she had to fly home again.

It was a call about a seminar in Seattle that Marco had said he would attend. Charlie tuned out after the first few minutes.

He put the phone down and raked one hand through the darkness of his hair. 'Sorry about that,' he said distractedly.

She shrugged. 'You'd better hurry and get ready if we are to be on time for dinner.'

'Yes.' He glanced at his watch. 'I'll have a quick shower. I won't be long. How's Jack, by the way?'

'He's fine. He's staying at Karen's because Mum is away for a few days with some friends.'

'Is he OK about moving?'

'I haven't told him yet.'

She saw his eyebrows rise. 'I'll tell him when I get home,' she added quickly.

He nodded and moved through towards the bedroom. Marco was right to look surprised, she supposed. She probably should have told Jack about her plans last week. But something had stopped her.

Charlie flicked through the TV channels and tried not to think too deeply about some of the doubts that had beset her last week. Every relationship was a risk. Even if Marco had declared undying love, moving in with him would still be a risk. The fact that he hadn't shouldn't really have mattered. Marco had said in his book that love would grow if you worked at it. And maybe that was what would happen between them.

She suddenly noticed with a start of surprise that she was looking at Marco on the TV screen. He looked fantastic, like a movie star about to discuss his latest part.

'You're on TV,' she called out.

'It will be a re-run of the Ed Johnson chat show. They keep showing it,' Marco called back as he disappeared through to the bathroom.

Charlie listened to the interview with interest. Ed Johnson was good at what he did and the show was intelligent as well as light-hearted. They touched on Marco's roots in Italy, his education and his past books, before dwelling more intently on his current book that was swiftly climbing the American charts. Marco was fantastic, entertaining, funny, very charismatic. He gave an account of his theories in a way that was serious yet very engaging. It was no wonder he was so much in demand and had achieved celebrity status.

'So basically what you are telling us is that the old saying about love being blind is true?' Ed Johnson asked.

'That's exactly right,' Marco agreed smoothly. 'You have to discount the feeling when looking for serious commitment. Of course, it's great to be in love, we all know that, and if the passion is there between you that's fantastic. But the feeling of love itself can be an illusion…you can think yourself in love or imagine that feeling is there because you really want it to be. And sometimes by the time you realise the mistake it's too late and you are heading for the divorce courts. That's why when you are looking for a long-term relationship you've got to look deeper than just emotional feelings. In fact, it's preferable to be best friends rather than to be deeply in love…'

'So where does your relationship fit with your theories?' Ed asked suddenly. 'Because I believe you have a new girlfriend in your life, and that the relationship is serious.'

'That's right. Charlie has been my PA for nearly six months now and we have been steadily getting closer over that time.'

She had heard Marco discussing his theories many times but it was really strange listening to him discussing their relationship. Even though she tried to tell herself that this was just a light TV programme, Charlie started to feel oddly vulnerable as she listened.

'So how close are you planning to get?' Ed asked.

'We're planning to move in together when I get back to England.'

The audience applauded wildly.

'And how does your relationship with Charlie compare to your theories?' Ed asked suddenly. 'Is this a love match or are you practising what you preach, so to speak?'

Charlie found herself moving forward on the sofa, her breath catching in her throat as she waited for the answer.

'Charlie and I work together well and we have a bond that is incredibly strong. In practical terms as a couple we tick all the right boxes.'

'So is this a love match?' Ed pressed for his answer.

'This is a match where neither of us have unrealistic expectations, we are on the same wavelength. We are willing to compromise. We're great friends and that's better than any unrealistic love match.'

Charlie felt suddenly sick. It was one thing telling herself that she could live without wild declarations of love, it was another thing entirely hearing the man she adored, the man she was about to move in with and dedicate her life to, describe her as merely his friend!

The phone rang, distracting her. 'Can you get that, Charlie?' Marco shouted from the other room.

She stood up and switched off the TV. She had heard enough.

She couldn't say that she was surprised by what she had

heard, because she had always known that was the truth. As far as Marco was concerned, they worked well together and 'they ticked all the right boxes'. They had passion, they had friendship but as for 'love'—well, apparently that was something you worked at…and maybe it was even an unnecessary emotion.

She hadn't expected anything more. And yet…the ache of disappointment and hurt was incredibly intense.

What if Marco *never* felt the same intensity of emotion for her as she did for him? She could wait and wait and it might never happen. The thought brought a chill deep inside.

'Charlie, are you going to get that phone?' Marco called again.

She picked it up impatiently. It was the chauffeur, who was waiting for them in the lobby, ready to take them for dinner.

'It's our driver,' she told Marco as he came through from the bedroom. He looked so handsome in his dark dinner suit and white shirt that she felt the lump in her throat grow.

'Right.' Marco looked at his watch. 'I suppose we will have to leave now.'

The last thing Charlie wanted was to go and have dinner with a room full of strangers, especially of people who had probably watched that interview. She was sure they would look at her and know the truth, know that her handsome lover didn't love her at all and that it was just a relationship of convenience.

With difficulty she forced herself to bury her smarting and crushed emotions. She had known the score when she had made her agreement with Marco. She couldn't start backing out of their agreement at this stage. For one thing, Marco was depending on her for the positive PR spin on his book. And for another, what could she say? Marco had never lied to her…he had never promised her love…and he didn't deserve for her to let him down now!

But could she really carry on with this and move in with

him? Did she really know what she was doing? The question pierced through her.

The large ballroom was filled with hundreds of people. The glitter of chandeliers dazzled over the diamonds and finery that the women wore. Charlie was very glad that she had splashed out on her sophisticated new evening dress.

She was horrified to find that Sarah Heart was attending the dinner. As soon as she and Marco stepped into the room Charlie saw her standing by the door, talking to a group of people. The woman looked stunning in a long red dress, her dark hair woven back from her face into a style that showed her classical bone structure and long neck to perfection.

'You didn't tell me that she was going to be here!' Charlie said in a low tone.

'Didn't I?' Marco shrugged. 'Sarah also represents Karina Kaplinski, so she's over here to do some promotional work for her as well.'

Charlie swallowed down a feeling of distaste. She may have disliked Sarah Heart intensely but she had very high-profile clients. Karina Kaplinski was a high-flying actress who had just written a sizzling autobiography that had taken the media by storm.

'That's Karina over there.' Marco nodded towards a beautiful, flame-haired woman in a long black dress.

As if sensing Marco's eyes on her, the woman turned and smiled at him and then blew him a kiss.

'Another one of your fans, I see,' Charlie remarked with a smile.

Marco laughed. 'We were on the same chat show last week. She's very theatrical.'

It wasn't long before Sarah was winging her way across the room towards them. 'Darling, how lovely to see you,' she gushed as she reached to kiss him on each cheek. 'And Charlie...' She turned to look towards her and seemed to do a double take as she took in her appearance. 'It's great you could make it.'

The welcome held a slight edge of insincerity, but then Charlie was surprised Sarah even acknowledged her. Usually she totally ignored her as if she didn't exist.

'Did you have a good journey?' Sarah asked solicitously.

This was even weirder, Charlie thought. Sarah rarely if ever tried to make any polite conversation with her. 'Yes, thank you.'

'Wonderful. Well, shall we take our seats for dinner?' Sarah smiled at Marco. 'As luck would have it we are sitting next to each other, Marco.'

Some things never changed, Charlie thought wryly.

They were seated at a table towards the front of the ballroom. Charlie found herself placed opposite Marco's editor, Jeffery Green, a tall, rather distinguished-looking man in his late fifties who had a thick head of grey hair and a twinkle in his blue eyes.

Karina Kaplinski was also at the table. She didn't so much make conversation but hold court over the long table. In particular she kept trying to get Marco's opinion on everything from the weather to the state of the nation and it didn't seem to matter to her that Charlie was sitting next to him because she flirted outrageously with him.

Marco took it all in his stride and just seemed lazily amused by her.

Jeffery smiled over at Charlie as Karina paused to draw breath. 'Great news about Marco's book.'

'What news is that?' Charlie asked.

'Oh, hasn't he told you? It made number one in the American bestseller charts two days ago.'

'Really? That's wonderful.' Charlie looked over at Marco and wondered why he hadn't told her when they had spoken on the phone. 'Congratulations.'

He smiled at her. 'Thanks.'

'I can't believe you didn't tell Charlie that!' She could hear Sarah's low whisper to Marco as the lights in the room suddenly started to lower, signalling that the meal had come to a close and the speeches were ready to begin. 'Don't forget, she's supposed to be your partner.'

Supposed to be your partner. The mocking words echoed inside Charlie as the music from the stage area started to blare, drowning out whatever Marco's reply had been. Then the compère for the evening walked out towards the podium.

She saw Karina lean across the table towards Marco and say something. She was probably propositioning him, safe in the knowledge that his *supposed partner* was no real competition.

Charlie didn't think for one minute that Marco was sexually interested in Karina or, for that matter, in Sarah. But what would happen when a woman came along who did interest him?

The question reverberated painfully through her mind.

It was all very well having this practical relationship based on friendship, but what happened when some woman really blew Marco and all his logical theories away? It was bound to happen one day because he was like a walking magnet for women. One day that special someone would come along and then where would their comfortable, practical relationship be?

She suddenly found herself remembering the last painful stages of her marriage when Greg told her he was leaving her and that he loved someone else.

She couldn't bear to go through something like that again.

Marco leaned closer and she could smell his cologne, which was tantalisingly provocative.

'Are you OK?' His voice was a whisper close against her ear.

'Yes.' She forced herself to smile. 'It's great news about your book.'

'Yes; thanks for your help with the PR side of things.' He kissed the side of her face. The casual kiss made her hurt inside as if someone had put a tight band around her heart and was squeezing it hard.

She could put up with Sarah's jibes…she could even put up with Marco speaking about their relationship in cool, business-like terms, but what she couldn't live with was the knowledge that one day Marco would leave her just the way Greg had, without so much as a backward glance.

She should never have weakened and said she'd move in with him. It had been a terrible mistake. The realisation hit her like a physical blow.

'And now a man who needs no introduction from me other than to say we have an eminent doctor in the house.' The loud tones of the compère rang through the auditorium. 'Ladies and gentlemen, please put your hands together for Dr Marco Delmari.'

Charlie watched as Marco walked up towards the stage. She listened to the thunderous applause and saw the way he handled it with that relaxed charm of his.

As he made a speech and then moved on towards handing out some award, Sarah moved into his empty seat and leaned across to speak to her. 'He's incredible, isn't he?' she said with a smile. 'This tour is going so well.'

'Yes, so it seems,' Charlie answered, wishing Sarah would move away. The last thing she needed right now was snide comments from her.

'Sorry if you were upset by what I said to you in Italy,' Sarah whispered suddenly.

'You didn't upset me.'

'Really? Marco thinks I did. But how was I supposed to know that he was going to carry this loveless-relationship idea to such lengths? Anyway, no hard feelings and I hope it works out for you.'

She moved back to her own seat as Marco started to leave the stage.

Charlie bit down on her lip. Sarah was such a horrible person, she'd just had to rub it in about their relationship being a sham. Although there wasn't much she could have replied to that because what Sarah had said was true.

Marco returned to his seat as the lights came on in the room. An orchestra started to play and a few couples went out onto the floor to dance to a smoothly romantic melody.

'Great speech, Marco,' Karina said silkily.

'Thanks.'

'Would you like to dance?' she invited softly.

'Sorry, not right now—I've got some catching up to do with Charlie.' He softened the refusal with a smile. 'Maybe later.'

'I'll hold you to that,' she practically purred and then turned to talk to a crowd of people who had come over to speak to her.

Marco turned back towards Charlie. 'I don't know about you but I could do with getting out of here,' he muttered.

'Yes, me too.'

'There are some people I have to see…' he looked around the room '…but once I've had a few words we'll escape.' He looked back at her. 'Do you want a dance first?'

'No, thanks, Marco, I'm a bit tired.' She didn't think she could handle going into his arms right now. She felt as if she had been on enough of an emotional roller coaster for one evening.

'Sorry! I keep forgetting you've had such a long journey today.' Marco glanced at his watch. 'What was Sarah saying to you, by the way?' he asked as he looked up.

The sudden question took her by surprise. 'Nothing much.'

'Well, she was saying something. I hope she wasn't stirring it again.'

'No…well, unless you count wishing us well in our loveless

relationship.' She tried to sound as if she was merely amused but the tone of her voice was more brittle than she had wanted.

Marco looked annoyed. 'She can't shut up, can she?'

'She was only speaking the truth. Neither of us have a right to be annoyed about that, have we?'

There was an uncomfortable silence between them for a moment.

'Charlie, I—'

'Let's not talk about it now, OK?' she cut across him breathlessly and her eyes blazed suddenly with unshed tears. If he said one word to defend their 'practical' relationship right now she knew she would break down.

He frowned. 'You're having second thoughts about us, aren't you?'

'Let's just get through this charade first, shall we?' Her voice was stiff. She really wanted to cry and she couldn't bear to do that here in front of him and all these people.

Someone stopped by the table to talk to Marco and as soon as he was distracted she took the opportunity to get up and move away. The room was packed and it was an effort to make her way towards the ladies'. Then she saw an exit door and headed for that instead.

What she needed was some fresh air and some space to clear her head.

After the crowded heat of the ballroom it was a relief when she got outside onto the pavement.

She took deep gulps of the cold night air. And then she tried to get things in perspective. She had done a lot of travelling today and she was probably over-tired and over-emotional.

Crowds swirled around her and, although she was outside in a flimsy evening dress, no one paid her any attention. It was as if she wasn't there.

A couple walked by, wrapped in each other's arms. The guy was looking at his girlfriend with rapt attention. That was what she wanted, she thought suddenly, someone who would look at her with that level of adoration…someone who really loved her.

She realised with a rush that she wasn't merely over-tired and that she was thinking more clearly than she had in weeks. She couldn't play this game of pretence with Marco. It hurt too much.

Before she could stop to analyse her actions she stepped forward. There was a yellow cab coming up the street and she flagged it down.

CHAPTER THIRTEEN

ONCE she was in the taxi she tried to phone Marco on his mobile but it was switched off and she just got his messaging service.

'Hi, it's me.' She tried to sound composed but there was such a fierce pain inside her chest from the weight of emotion she carried that it was hard to even speak. 'Look, I realise by rushing off like this that I'm behaving very badly and…probably erratically. I'm sorry,' she drew in her breath, 'but I can't go through with this, Marco. I realised tonight that it just wouldn't work between us. I'm heading back to the hotel and I'm going to pack my stuff and check out. I think it's for the best. I hope you'll forgive me.'

She hung up and put the phone back in her bag.

The words rang hollow inside her but she knew despite the pain that she had done the right thing. Better to end things now than to let them get too far out of hand.

She had learnt her lesson with Greg. She couldn't go through that again. And it could be even worse with Marco…she was so head-over-heels in love with him it was crazy.

The cab pulled up outside her hotel and she paid the driver and hurried inside. She needed to pack and get out of this hotel before Marco got back. If he started to try and persuade her to stay she knew she would get emotional and say things she didn't want to say.

At least if she got away now she would have time to pull herself together and when she did speak to him again she could try and exit from his life with some scrap of dignity.

As soon as she got back into their suite she took out her suitcase and opened it on the bed. Then she took off her dress and put on her jeans and a T-shirt before throwing everything else into the case.

The trouble with not taking the time to fold things was that the case then refused to close. After the fourth attempt she finally got the locks closed and picked it up. And that was when she heard the door open.

Her heart thundered erratically as she turned and came face to face with Marco.

'What the hell are you playing at?' His dark gaze moved from her towards the suitcase.

She took a deep breath. 'I'm really sorry, Marco. Did you get my message?'

He tossed his mobile phone down on the table. 'Yes, and it made about as much sense as seeing you standing there with your suitcase. Where do you think you are going?'

'I'm going to check into another hotel.'

'Why?'

She shrugged helplessly. 'I told you on the phone. I realise I've made a mistake. I can't move in with you, Marco. So I think it's best I leave.'

He watched the way she held her head high, the spark of defiance in her eye.

'You don't really need me here now anyway. I've done what you needed. Plus your book is number one in the charts, so it's OK.'

'No, it's not OK,' he cut across her firmly. 'Look, you are over-tired, you've had a long day and now you've just got a classic case of cold feet.'

'Well, thanks for the diagnosis, Doctor, but you're wrong.'

His calm manner irritated her. 'You talked me into moving in with you but I was never sure it was the right thing…and now I know it's not.'

'Really?' He crossed his arms. 'Because of some outrageous comment from Sarah Heart?'

'It wasn't an outrageous comment.' Her voice trembled slightly. 'It was true and you know it.'

He didn't say anything to that and she suddenly felt tears welling up inside her. 'I'm not leaving just because of Sarah's comments, it's more complicated than that.'

'What's that supposed to mean?'

When she made no reply he muttered fiercely, 'I think I deserve more of an explanation than that. Don't you?'

'Well, for a start, there was your TV interview.' She shrugged helplessly.

'What about it?'

The calm question made her temper flare. The hurt feelings that she had been trying so hard to rein in since she had listened to that interview started to spill out. 'You mean apart from the fact that you told the whole world that you and I are just some kind of experiment in relationship terms?'

'Don't be absurd!'

'That's what you said more or less. That you are with me to prove your point about love not being necessary.' She put her hand on her hip. 'Well, I've decided that you can go and prove your point with someone else.'

'Charlie, I haven't asked you to move in with me to prove a point.' His voice softened.

'Well, you could have fooled me!'

'You are being totally irrational,' he said with a frown.

'Am I?' She glared at him. 'Well, I did try to warn you that we are not as compatible as you thought,' she blazed furiously, 'because the fact is that I can be wildly illogical when I want to be.'

'Really?' Instead of looking annoyed he seemed briefly amused.

'Just move out of my way, Marco—I want to leave.' She took a few steps forward towards the door but he made no attempt to move out of her way and he looked very serious now.

'I'm sorry, Charlie, but there is no way I am allowing you to leave,' he said softly. 'Not until I know exactly what the hell you are talking about.'

'Well, let me make it clear, Marco: I really thought I could live a life with you that didn't involve love but I just can't.'

'Love will grow between us,' he said gently. 'I know it will.'

She shook her head and tears threatened to spill now. 'I can't take that chance, Marco. It hurts too much when everything goes wrong.'

He moved across to her and took her suitcase from unresisting fingers. Then he pulled her close and held her.

For a moment she allowed herself to lean against him and the feeling was blissful.

'Everything won't go wrong between us.' His voice was low and reassuring. 'We are good together. You know that deep down.'

'But it's not enough.' She pulled away from him. It felt so good to be in his arms but she couldn't allow herself to be swayed by emotions that weren't real. That was what always happened when she was around him and it was a dangerous distraction.

'But you said you wanted companionship and stability and we can have all that—'

'It's not enough, Marco,' she cut across him with raw emphasis. 'And I'm sorry I led you to believe otherwise.' She swallowed hard. 'You once told me I was too emotional to ever be happy with that kind of arrangement and you were right. You should have gone with your first analysis of me.'

When he didn't say anything to that she looked up at him with shimmering eyes. 'It's not that I don't believe in your theories about working at a relationship, because I do.' Her voice became a mere whisper. 'But, you see, for me love is the building block, the starting point, and without it there's really *no* point.' She bit down on her lip.

'So you couldn't learn to love me, then?' he asked quietly.

The husky words made her heart suddenly miss several beats. She wanted to tell him that she already did love him, but pride made the words stick in her throat.

She couldn't meet his eye now. 'I think it's just best that I go and we call it a day. Don't worry, we can keep it quiet from the media—'

'To hell with the media, Charlie, I really couldn't care less about it,' he grated angrily.

She frowned. 'Well, of course you care. Your book and your work is all-important to you.'

'Not as important as you.'

Charlie had been in the process of turning away but she paused in her tracks.

'Don't go, Charlie…please.'

Her heart stopped for a second at that husky, uncertain tone that was so unlike him.

'Do you know why I didn't tell you that my book was number one in the American chart?' he asked abruptly. 'Because it meant that in practical terms I didn't need you here…the book was doing well and I was doing fine without a partner by my side.'

She frowned, not following what he meant.

'I didn't want to tell you because I thought it would give you an excuse not to come,' he continued bluntly. 'And the truth was that I needed you…'

'You did?'

He nodded. 'I missed you so much that it hurt. I love you, Charlie.'

The admission made her whirl around to face him, her eyes wide.

'Is this some sort of game?' she whispered.

'Yes, it's called the truth game.' Marco's lips twisted derisively. 'Look, I've tried to take things slowly so as not to scare you off. But I can't let you go.'

She took a tentative step towards him. 'Say that again,' she whispered.

'I can't let you go.' He reached out and touched her face. 'Because I love you.'

She could hardly believe what he was saying to her.

'In fact, I love everything about you,' he added softly. 'The way you wear your hair—whether it is tied up or left loose,' he added. 'With or without glasses…in evening dress or even wrapped in a towel.' He gave a helpless kind of shrug.

She stared at him in a sense of wonderment. 'I thought I was just a "friend" who ticked all the right boxes?'

'A friend who I fell in love with,' he corrected softly. 'Look, I know you don't feel the same but it will grow…I know it will, because that's what happened to me. When I came back from Italy I realised how deeply I felt for you and that I just couldn't live without you. The debacle with the photographers in Florence made me recognize that I never wanted any hurt to come to you ever again. I tried to deny the feelings but…' he shrugged helplessly '…some things just can't be denied. And if you just give me a chance to prove myself to you I know I can make you happy.

'Charlie, don't cry!' He looked appalled as he saw huge tears spilling down her face and pulled her into his arms. 'God, it tears me apart, seeing you like this.'

'I'm OK,' she murmured huskily.

'No, you're not, and it's my fault. I tried to rush you into moving in with me because I couldn't bear not to have you in my life. But I should have taken things slower, given you time to get used to the idea, time to think about us as a family—'

'I don't need more time…not now—'

'Just give things a little longer,' he cut across her earnestly. 'We'll take things slow. I'll do whatever it takes—'

'Marco, I don't need to take things slowly.' She looked up at him. 'Because I already love you; I always have.'

She saw the look of surprise in his expression. And then suddenly she was in his arms and he was kissing her with a passion that made her breathless. She clung to him and melted into him, her body tingling with happiness and exhilaration.

'Charlie, when you told me you couldn't live without love I honestly thought you were going to walk out. I've always prided myself on the fact that I look at situations in a rational way…but God, I couldn't bear to lose you.'

The rawness in his eyes made her realise how completely she had broken through his defences. 'I meant I couldn't live without your love for me,' she corrected him softly.

A smile started to curve Marco's lips.

He reached out and touched the side of her face, a look of perplexity in his eyes. 'I've always sensed such wariness in you. In fact, I thought that you might not be over your ex-husband.'

'I was over Greg a long time ago. If I was wary it was because I don't want to go through the heartache of another break-up.'

He nodded. 'I can understand that. But I have to admit, when you talked about just wanting companionship and prac-ticalities for your next relationship…I thought it meant he was still in your heart.'

'The only person in my heart was you, Marco.' She swallowed hard. 'I lied about all that anyway. And I think I did it because I've always been in love with you…and I didn't think you would ever feel the same way about me. Even when you asked me to move in with you I thought it was for purely practical reasons, because I'm good in the office, because we get on well…'

'Well, that last bit is true, of course,' Marco said teasingly.

'Marco!' She looked up at him reproachfully and he kissed her. It was a kiss that was so sweetly full of emotion she could feel his love like a tangible force inside her.

'I would have thought kisses like that might have told you something else,' he murmured as he pulled back.

'I thought you were just good at passion because you are Italian,' she said with a smile.

He laughed at that.

'I've never kissed anyone the way I've kissed you.' He looked deep into her eyes. 'And I'm not talking about the fact that we are good in bed together…which we most definitely are. I'm talking about the way you make me feel in here.' He put a hand on his chest. 'You've touched my heart the way no one has ever done.'

'Do you realise that is the most romantic thing anyone has ever said to me?' she said teasingly. 'And this from the man who shuns sentimentality of any sort.'

'It just happens to be true. So it's not sentimental slush!'

She smiled at him. 'God, I love you, Marco…'

'Does that mean you will move in with me?'

'Of course it does.'

For a long while they didn't speak and just kissed. They were the most blissfully happy moments of Charlie's life.

'When you move in it's for keeps, Charlie,' he told her firmly as he pulled away. 'In sickness and health, for richer or poorer…all of that.'

'All of that,' she agreed softly. 'So what's happened to the inveterate bachelor…the guy who wasn't cut out for commitment?' she asked with a smile.

'He just found the right woman.'

Marco's lips crushed against hers in a kiss of such tenderness that it took her breath away.

'And who would have thought that the woman in question was an incurable romantic?' she murmured as she wound her arms up and around his neck. 'Did I tell you that I fell in love with you at first sight, by the way?'

'Sorry to disappoint you, but that was just lust, Charlie,' Marco laughed, and picked her up to carry her back towards the bed.

She didn't argue…but she knew he was wrong about that.

HARLEQUIN *Presents*

EXTRA

HIRED: FOR THE BOSS'S PLEASURE

She's gone from personal assistant to mistress—but now he's demanding she become the boss's bride!

Read all our fabulous stories this month:

MISTRESS: HIRED FOR THE BILLIONAIRE'S PLEASURE
by INDIA GREY

THE BILLIONAIRE BOSS'S INNOCENT BRIDE
by LINDSAY ARMSTRONG

HER RUTHLESS ITALIAN BOSS
by CHRISTINA HOLLIS

MEDITERRANEAN BOSS, CONVENIENT MISTRESS
by KATHRYN ROSS

HPE0209

HARLEQUIN *Presents*

International Billionaires

*Life is a game of power and pleasure.
And these men play to win!*

AT THE ARGENTINIAN BILLIONAIRE'S BIDDING
by India Grey

Billionaire Alejandro D'Arienzo desires revenge
on Tamsin—the heiress who wrecked his past.
Tamsin is shocked when Alejandro threatens her
business with his ultimatum: *her name in tatters
or her body in his bed...*
Book #2806

Available March 2009

Eight volumes in all to collect!

HARLEQUIN *Presents*

*Introducing an exciting debut
from Harlequin Presents!*

Indulge yourself with this intense story
of passion, blackmail and seduction.

VALENTI'S
ONE-MONTH MISTRESS
by Sabrina Philips

Faye fell for the sensual Dante Valenti—but he
took her virginity and left her heartbroken. She
swore *never again!* But he wants her back,
and what Dante wants, Dante takes....

Book #2808

Available March 2009

Look out for more titles from Sabrina Philips
coming soon to Harlequin Presents!

REQUEST YOUR FREE BOOKS!

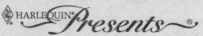 

2 FREE NOVELS
PLUS 2
FREE GIFTS!

YES! Please send me 2 FREE Harlequin Presents® novels and my 2 FREE gifts (gifts are worth about $10). After receiving them, if I don't wish to receive any more books, I can return the shipping statement marked "cancel." If I don't cancel, I will receive 6 brand-new novels every month and be billed just $4.05 per book in the U.S. or $4.74 per book in Canada, plus 25¢ shipping and handling per book and applicable taxes, if any*. That's a savings of close to 15% off the cover price! I understand that accepting the 2 free books and gifts places me under no obligation to buy anything. I can always return a shipment and cancel at any time. Even if I never buy another book, the two free books and gifts are mine to keep forever.

106 HDN ERRW   306 HDN ERRL

Name	(PLEASE PRINT)	
Address		Apt. #
City	State/Prov.	Zip/Postal Code

Signature (if under 18, a parent or guardian must sign)

Mail to the **Harlequin Reader Service:**
IN U.S.A.: P.O. Box 1867, Buffalo, NY 14240-1867
IN CANADA: P.O. Box 609, Fort Erie, Ontario L2A 5X3

Not valid to current subscribers of Harlequin Presents books.

Want to try two free books from another line?
Call 1-800-873-8635 or visit www.morefreebooks.com.

* Terms and prices subject to change without notice. N.Y. residents add applicable sales tax. Canadian residents will be charged applicable provincial taxes and GST. Offer not valid in Quebec. This offer is limited to one order per household. All orders subject to approval. Credit or debit balances in a customer's account(s) may be offset by any other outstanding balance owed by or to the customer. Please allow 4 to 6 weeks for delivery. Offer available while quantities last.

Your Privacy: Harlequin Books is committed to protecting your privacy. Our Privacy Policy is available online at www.eHarlequin.com or upon request from the Reader Service. From time to time we make our lists of customers available to reputable third parties who may have a product or service of interest to you. If you would prefer we not share your name and address, please check here.

HP08R

HARLEQUIN *Presents*

ONE NIGHT BABY

When passion leads to pregnancy!

PLEASURE, PREGNANCY AND A PROPOSITION
by Heidi Rice

With tall, sexy, gorgeous men like these,
it's easy to get carried away with
the passion of the moment—and end up
unexpectedly, accidentally, shockingly

PREGNANT!

Book #2809

Available March 2009

Don't miss any books in this exciting new
miniseries from Harlequin Presents!

I ♥ HARLEQUIN Presents

BROUGHT TO YOU BY FANS OF
HARLEQUIN PRESENTS.

We are its editors and authors
and biggest fans—and we'd
love to hear from YOU!

Subscribe today to our online blog at
www.iheartpresents.com